THE NIGHT THE BABY-SITTER DIDN'T COME

Other Apple paperbacks
you will enjoy:

Camp Trouble
by Beverly Keller

Why Would Anyone Have a Crush on Horace Beemis?
by Jacqueline Shannon

Our Teacher Is Missing
by Mary Francis Shura

Sixth-Grade High
by Candice F. Ransom

Shoebag
by Mary James

A Ghost in the House
by Betty Ren Wright

Why Me?
by Deborah Kent

THE NIGHT THE BABY-SITTER DIDN'T COME

Beverly Keller

SCHOLASTIC INC.
New York Toronto London Auckland Sydney

ISBN 0-590-43726-7

12 11 10 9 8 7 6 5 4 3 2 4 5 6 7 8 9/9

Printed in the U.S.A. 40

First Scholastic printing, May 1994

THE NIGHT THE BABY-SITTER DIDN'T COME

1

"How could you do this to me?" Phoebe Townsend-Fanchon cried.

Brian Fanchon, Phoebe's father, reached across the table to pat her hand, trailing the cuff of his Italian silk shirt over his Amaranth Crunch cereal. "Sweetheart, in a civilized world we do favors for our neighbors."

"Sure, if they have civilized kids." Phoebe could see that her father was not going to respond to cries of outrage — the only thing left was to act quietly but desperately miserable.

Iris Townsend, her mother, calmly poured Phoebe a glass of Eden Soy, cartons of which had been a special at the food co-op. "Angel, that is a hurtful thing to say. Besides, you told us you had a lovely time with Heather and Tiffany at camp."

Phoebe took a deep breath and forced herself to let it out slowly, with only the slightest groan. "I *said* it wasn't *horrible*, but they still act as if being two years older than me . . ."

"Two years older than I," Brian corrected her.

"Okay. They act as if being twelve makes them *better* than me . . . than I."

Brian slit open a tiny carton of mandarin-lime juice that came from a bin of closeout merchandise at Pier One and put it in front of Phoebe. "Ten is a wonderful age. You should enjoy it!"

Phoebe knew that if she asked him whether he had enjoyed being ten, he would tell her about all the hours he spent at that age practicing the violin. "Suppose I try my best to enjoy being ten, and you let me out of spending the weekend with Heather and Tiffany," she proposed.

Iris poured hot water from a carafe over the metal ball filled with Lapsang-souchong tea in the glazed pot. "Precious, you and Tiffany are going to spend Saturday night at Heather's, because that way, their parents won't have to hire a sitter for tonight, and we won't have to hire a sitter for tomorrow night."

"Why can't Tiffany stay at Heather's tonight? They could at least afford to share a sitter for one night."

Iris flicked a bit of mango chutney off the table. "Tiffany's mother said the two girls had a little falling out."

"Sure," Phoebe said. "That's because nobody in her right mind could stand either of them. So then they both get dumped on us, right?"

"That's right," Brian Fanchon said firmly.

"Heather and Tiffany spend tonight here and you all spend tomorrow night at Heather's. That is known as cooperation."

That is also known as stiffing a sitter, Phoebe thought. But she did not say so. Brian was a gentle man, but the tone of his voice made it clear that Phoebe had pushed him as far as he was willing to be pushed.

Still, the prospect of two nights with Tiffany and Heather was so ghastly, Phoebe could not endure it without a last, hopeless struggle. "How about you hire a sitter for Tiffany and Heather tonight, and for me tomorrow night? You can keep my allowances until it's paid for."

"Now, that is absurd," Iris declared. "It is also unspeakably insulting to the Bowens and the Reillys. Heather's parents have hired a highly reliable girl for tomorrow night."

"So how about just getting somebody for me so I can stay home tomorrow?" There was no harm in offering to compromise. She knew this was financially shaky, since Saturday would be the first concert her parents had played in weeks, and when they weren't playing concerts, they had to live off credit cards. They already owed Phoebe three weeks' back allowance. If they could pay me by credit card they probably would, she thought.

"You know the luck we've had with sitters," Brian added darkly.

There was no hope, then. Heather and Tiffany

would be spending the night, and she would be stuck at Heather's the next night.

Phoebe poured a little Eden Soy into her Back to Nature Sprouted Seven Grain Fiber cereal. The little brown nuggets looked like dog kibble. Even though her parents had remained fairly calm and reasonable through the short skirmish they'd just had with her, Phoebe knew their patience might be strained enough to snap if she were to bring up the fact that her cereal looked like dog food.

Still, she couldn't help thinking that other ten-year-olds probably got regular cereals like Shredded Wheat or sugarcoated pastel colored loops. Other parents shopped at supermarkets, and paid by cash or checks. They got regular paychecks instead of playing piano and violin concerts all over the state and getting paid only after they played. Other parents didn't keep running out of money so they had to buy groceries at whatever places took credit cards.

Other parents had relatives, too. Heather and Tiffany each had four grandparents, and aunts and uncles and cousins, even second and third cousins. All Phoebe had was one grandmother — a grandmother who had a gentleman friend. Phoebe was sure nobody she knew had a grandmother who *dated.*

Tonight Tiffany's parents were going to some aunt's wedding out of the state. Tiffany didn't seem insulted not to be invited. "My aunt said that if I came, they'd have to invite all the kids in the family, and they'd have a madhouse instead of a wedding."

Imagine, Phoebe thought, having enough cousins to destroy a wedding. And tomorrow night, Heather's parents were going with a bunch of people to the Monterey Pop festival. Not my parents, Phoebe reflected. My parents only play classical concerts. My parents have probably never even been to a rock concert. We are so out of it!

The telephone rang.

"I'll get it." Phoebe hurried to answer. Maybe it was Heather or Tiffany calling to say she'd come down with a virus and everybody's weekend plans were off.

It was Amy Rivas, Phoebe's best friend from summer camp — the first long distance call Phoebe had ever received.

"Listen," Amy said, "I just talked my folks into letting me go to the county fair *without* them! Every year, they drag me along. But not this time! So, can you come?"

This was more exciting than anybody's virus. "What county fair?"

"San Mateo."

Phoebe's excitement died. "That's down the Peninsula."

"Only about thirty miles from you."

There was nothing to do but confess it. "Amy, my mother and father don't drive. We don't even have a car."

Amy didn't seem shocked. One of the great things about Amy was that she ignored any opportunity to put people down. "So you can take the train."

"From San Francisco?"

"Sure. We could pick you up at the station here. It's just a few blocks from the fairgrounds. The fair will be great — rides and games and food and exhibits and stage shows and everything."

"Hold on and I'll ask!"

"If I hold on, my mom's going to start fussing that this is a long distance call. First get your folks to say okay, and then have your mom call mine and work out the train schedules and stuff."

"How much money will I need?"

"I don't know. I'll probably get fifteen dollars to spend. And if you're really short, I could treat you to some things."

Phoebe wasn't sure her parents had fifteen dollars to spare. On the other hand, shouldn't they make some sacrifices for a child who had lived ten years and had never seen a county fair?

2

"Absolutely not." Iris Townsend squirted Aloe Vera dishwashing liquid into the pan and stepped to one side so Brian could open the cupboard door under the sink.

"Mother!" Phoebe cried. "It may be the only chance I'll ever get to go to a county fair. I'll give up my allowance for a *month* . . ."

"It's not the money," Brian said. "Have you forgotten your guests?"

"Tiffany Reilly and Heather Bowen are not *my* guests."

"They are our guests, dear." Iris lowered the dishes into the pan.

"You'll be here," Phoebe pointed out.

"It's not the same." Iris was calm and implacable. "You are not going to take off and abandon them. Besides, I am not letting any child of mine take a public conveyance to San Mateo."

"Mother, it's probably only half an hour's ride!"

"And you are only ten years old." Brian lifted

the sack of garbage out of the rack and started for the back stairs, not noticing the drops of disgusting-looking stuff oozing from the bottom of the bag.

"So I'm supposed to tell Amy, my best friend in the world, that I can't come to probably the only fair I'll ever be invited to because I have to baby-sit Heather Bowen and Tiffany Reilly, and my parents are afraid of trains!"

"Don't talk too long," Iris told her. "It's a toll call."

Brian Fanchon walked out the back door, leaving a trail of garbage juice on the linoleum.

Phoebe went back to the telephone. She wanted to think Amy might say, "That's okay. Bring Heather and Tiffany." But she knew that was not going to happen. Even though Tiffany and Heather had stopped teasing Amy the last days at camp, they'd made her first days miserable. Of course, Phoebe had to admit, Amy was the kind of kid who attracted teasing.

Phoebe was right. Amy was disappointed. Amy was sympathetic.

Amy did not say, "Why don't you bring Heather and Tiffany?"

Phoebe went to her room to suffer.

Nobody noticed.

If I had brothers or sisters, she thought, at least one of them would go tell my parents I'm miserable.

At lunch, she barely picked at her soy-filled manicotti.

Nobody noticed.

She sighed.

Nobody glanced at her.

She ate her lunch.

Afterward, she helped clear the table, very slowly, like someone bearing a heavy burden.

She could see that her parents were not going to pick up on any body language.

"I was going to go to the library and take out some serious books," she said. "But, of course, with Tiffany and Heather here I suppose it would be rude to read."

"It would," her mother agreed — firmly.

After the dishes were done, Phoebe went to her room, hoping that she might come down with something contagious, but not seriously unpleasant, in the short time before Heather and Tiffany would arrive.

She was in the bathroom looking for a thermometer when she heard a knock at the apartment's front door.

She didn't even open the door to see who the caller was — until she recognized Mrs. Reilly's voice.

Phoebe hurried toward the living room. Maybe the Reillys had decided to take Tiffany to the wedding, invited or not. Maybe they had suddenly realized she was too obnoxious to wish on any neighbors.

Mrs. Reilly stood in the foyer, talking fast. "I don't know what we can do. My sister Grace and her husband had a sitter all lined up to stay with their son Dalton, but now the woman's sick, and they can't find anyone else. And of course, they can't take Dalton. They thought that if we had a sitter for Tiffany, they could leave Dalton at our house, but then I had to tell them that we were leaving her with you, and of course we couldn't expect you to take Dalton, too. So they're just going to call and cancel out, which is a shame, since that means having two catered dinners at the reception going to waste . . ."

"Don't worry." Iris Townsend sounded sympathetic, but not entirely convincing. "We'd be happy to have Dalton here."

"Oh, we couldn't do that." Mrs. Reilly sounded even less convincing than Iris. "Grace would never *dream* of imposing on you. Of course, Dalton is no trouble at all. The *quietest* child . . ."

"No, it's perfectly all right." Iris Townsend sounded as if she were trying to reassure someone who'd spilled coffee on the best rug. "We'll be glad to keep him."

"But then you *must* let us take Phoebe for you one weekend soon," Mrs. Reilly said fervently.

Phoebe backed down the hall to her room. What can you do with parents who invite not only the world's most obnoxious twelve-year-olds for the weekend, but a kid they hadn't even *seen*! He could be an arsonist, a shoplifter! Maybe he was quiet because he had a lot to hide!

She heard Mrs. Reilly leave, and heard her parents talking together, their voices low and tense. Good, she thought. Let my father know what it feels like to have somebody you didn't invite dumped on you.

And then she was inspired. The weekend didn't have to be altogether hideous!

She padded to the kitchen phone.

She spoke barely loud enough to be heard. "Listen, Amy, how about you spending the weekend here?"

"When?" Amy sounded thrilled.

Amy probably didn't get asked many places by other kids, Phoebe realized. Amy was the kind who attracted tormenting, not invitations. "Right away."

"Great. I'd rather visit you than go to the fair." Then Amy sounded a little nervous. "Will Heather and Tiffany be there?"

"Yeah, but it's *my* house and I'm a lot tougher here than at camp." There was no need to explain that they'd be spending the next night at Heather's. Amy *needed* to get out more. There was no harm in putting off little details for Amy's own good.

Phoebe could tell that Amy was torn between being around Heather and Tiffany and going to a slumber party. "Is it okay with your parents?"

"No problem." After all, Phoebe thought, fair was fair. But would parents who refused to let their kid go to a fair see the justice in what she was doing? It would take all the reasonableness and pitifulness a kid possessed to pull this one off, she knew.

"Hold on!" Amy's voice was almost shivery with eagerness.

She came back to the phone in a minute. "My mom wants to know if your parents will be there."

"Sure." No sense getting into Saturday and all those complications. Besides, a responsible sitter was the same as a parent.

"My brother could drive me there. Then my dad could pick me up Sunday. He's been promising to take my mom to the city for brunch. So when should I come over?"

"Right away."

"Okay. I'll tell my brother, and then I just have to pack my stuff. Should I bring a sleeping bag?"

"Nah. Heather and Tiffany can bring theirs. You can have the other bed in my room."

"I'd better bring my sleeping bag. There's no point making either of them more hostile than nature did."

Phoebe strolled into the living room, where her mother was demanding of Brian, "What could I *do*?"

"Amy's coming, too," Phoebe announced casually.

Her parents stopped fussing at each other.

"Amy?" Brian looked at Iris.

"Amy?" Iris looked at Phoebe.

"Amy Rivas, my very best friend at camp."

"Coming where?" Brian asked.

"Over here." Phoebe managed to sound offhand.

"Who told you . . ." her mother began.

"I thought since you invited Tiffany and Heather to make my life miserable, and then, without even asking me, invited some little boy who will probably wreck all my favorite belongings and give me elsers — "

"Ulcers," Brian corrected her automatically.

Phoebe looked ever so slightly bewildered. "I thought you'd be happy."

"Happy?" Iris rasped.

Phoebe didn't wince. Phoebe spoke like a noble person who is constantly misunderstood. "Pleased that instead of sulking and complaining I invited somebody *I* like."

Iris was not moved. "Who gave you permission?"

Phoebe looked genuinely surprised. "Permission?"

It was time, Phoebe saw, for the big guns. "I thought, since I've always been an only child, if *I* could have a friend, someone I like, somebody who is nice to *me*, I would probably be so grateful I'd go out of my way to be nice to Heather and to Tiffany and her horrible little cousin."

"This is not worthy of you," Brian said sternly.

"This is blackmail," Iris declared.

Phoebe looked profoundly depressed.

Her parents looked at each other.

"You can't bring Amy to Heather's." Brian was firm. "You do not bring an extra person to somebody's house for the night."

Phoebe spoke like an attorney from a high-class television series. "But the Reillys wished an extra child on us. If they didn't think it was all right, they wouldn't do it, would they? And you wouldn't let them, would you?"

Iris looked at Brian. "Do you want to explain to her?"

"Do you?" he asked.

Phoebe went back to her room to struggle with mixed feelings. She was happy that Amy was coming, but worried about being a blackmailer. What if her parents were worried about having a child with criminal tendencies?

The idea of *being* a ten-year-old with a criminal mind made her feel as if cold lava were oozing into her stomach.

Would they send her to a psychiatrist? Would the psychiatrist advise them that she was bound to go bad no matter what?

Phoebe didn't even hurry out to answer the telephone when it rang again. Maybe Mrs. Reilly had remembered another relative who couldn't get a sitter.

Phoebe heard her mother answer, gasp, and then shout, "Brian!"

When Phoebe ran out into the hall, Iris was already putting on a sweater, and Brian was hanging up the telephone. Both of them looked pale and terribly, terribly calm.

"Call Tiffany's house," Iris told Phoebe. "If her parents haven't left already, tell them we have to rush out, but we'll be back as soon as possible."

Brian shrugged into a jacket.

"What is it?" Phoebe felt so scared she forgot she was resenting her parents.

"There's a fire at the warehouse," Iris said. "Keep all the doors locked. When Tiffany and her cousin and Heather come, let them in, but nobody else. And be sure who it is before you unlock the door!" She ran out the front door after Brian.

"Wait!" Phoebe had to open the door. "What about Amy?"

"Try to head her off." Brian didn't break his stride. "If it's too late, you'll have to let her in."

Iris was in the street, flagging down a taxi.

"Lock up!" Brian yelled at Phoebe.

Phoebe felt all shaky and sweaty as she dialed Amy's number.

"This is . . ." A man's voice recited Amy's telephone number and said nobody was available and invited the caller to leave a message after the beep.

Phoebe was not sure what to do. If nobody was

home to answer the Rivases' phone, it meant Amy was on her way. You couldn't tell somebody on her way to your house not to come.

By that time, she'd waited so long after the beep that it would sound peculiar to leave a message.

Besides, what message could she leave?

She felt guilty just hanging up, like an anonymous caller or something.

Phoebe punched in the Reillys' number.

"Have your folks gone yet?" she asked when Tiffany answered.

"Just a minute ago. I'm on my way over with old Dalton."

"Can you catch them?"

"No. Why?"

"Nothing. I'll see you. Be sure you both bring sleeping bags."

Phoebe hung up and sat shivering. A fire. She only hoped her father and mother would not try to run into the warehouse to rescue their piano.

She told herself to be reasonable. There was no way two people could carry a grand piano out of a burning warehouse. They'd surely be too sensible to try. Odd they might be, but not foolish. Besides, they were always careful not to hurt their hands.

She dialed the Bowens' number. She recognized Mrs. Bowen's taped voice telling her to leave a message. Since nobody was answering the phone, it must mean that Heather was on her way.

When she heard the knocking, she hurried to the door. "Who is it?"

"Who do you think, the bubonic plague or something?"

"Okay." Phoebe slid the chain free, pulled back the bolt, undid the lock in the knob and the one below it, and opened the door.

Tiffany walked in, carrying a small suitcase and a rolled-up sleeping bag. Behind her was a boy who looked about eight. He was slender, almost frail-looking, with soft, straight blond hair and gray eyes. Beside the pack and sleeping bag on his back, he was burdened by the large covered cage he carried in his arms.

"Why did you want my folks?" Tiffany demanded.

Phoebe gazed at the cage. She'd never seen a square bird cage before.

"Where do I put my stuff?" Tiffany pressed.

Phoebe led the way to her bedroom. Dalton might look gentle, even shy, but all her suspicions about him returned. How could anybody, even a kid, see birds soaring free and not realize how cruel it was to keep one behind bars?

Tiffany plopped her suitcase on one of the twin beds and dumped the sleeping bag on the floor. Dalton dropped his sleeping bag and backpack on top of it, set the cage on the other bed, and pulled off the cage cover.

"Oh, wow." Phoebe didn't want to sound scared.

Do that and Dalton would know how to torture me all weekend, she thought. "A rat."

"Her name's Rowena," Dalton confided. "Sean Livotnik's rat had a whole litter, and his parents made him give all the babies away."

Phoebe peered warily at Rowena. "This is not a baby rat. This is a very large rat."

"That's why Sean's parents made him give them all away. They were growing up."

Phoebe watched Rowena washing her face with her paws. "Nobody told my folks you were bringing . . ."

Tiffany shook her head. "He was supposed to leave the dumb thing at our house, but he wouldn't, even with plenty of food and water for her. He threw a wingding when I tried to make him."

Dalton looked at Phoebe, as if he knew she'd understand. "I can't leave her cooped up in a cage, all alone in a strange place. Besides, she's been acting twitchy."

"Twitchy?" Phoebe was sure her parents weren't prepared to have a rat guest for the weekend, let alone a twitchy one.

"She doesn't bite or anything." Dalton stuck his fingers between the wires and scratched Rowena's neck gently. "She just seems a little bit nervous."

There was a knock at the front door. "I'm not supposed to let anybody in unless it's Heather or . . . or somebody like that," Phoebe worried.

"If it's not who you're expecting, tell them your father is in the bathtub," Dalton volunteered. "That's what you're supposed to say when you're alone and anybody comes to the door."

Phoebe's parents had never left her alone in the apartment before. "I just go to the door and yell through it 'My father's in the bathtub'?"

Tiffany sighed. "Come on." At the front door, she called out, "Who is it?"

"Me." It was Heather.

Tiffany planted her fists on her hips. "Yeah?"

"I brought my boom box and my new tapes," Heather said through the door.

Phoebe was beginning to feel overwhelmed by all that had happened in a few minutes — her parents rushed to a fire in the warehouse; Tiffany showed up with her cousin and a rat; Amy was on her way; and now Heather Bowen was outside.

Edging around Tiffany, Phoebe unlocked the door.

Heather was holding a long lavender portable tape player in one hand, an overnight bag in the other, and a rolled sleeping bag under her arm.

Tiffany looked at her coldly. "I suppose you're going to try to make up."

Heather shrugged.

"You want to?" Tiffany looked at the cassette player.

Heather scratched at her nose with it. "I don't know. Do you?"

"I don't know. If you do. I guess. Maybe. What tapes did you bring?"

"Everything that drives my parents crazy."

Now is probably a good time to tell them Amy is coming, Phoebe thought. On the other hand, maybe she won't get here until my folks get back. Heather and Tiffany would never act truly rotten in front of parents.

3

While Heather and Tiffany didn't exactly *include* Phoebe, they didn't go out of their way to ignore her. They played tapes in Phoebe's room, with Rowena running up Dalton's arm and nibbling his neck. Phoebe was careful not to look at her, knowing that if she even seemed uneasy, Dalton would probably start pushing her to pet the rat.

There was enough worry wondering what was happening at the warehouse.

"Can't you put that thing in its cage?" Heather glowered at Rowena.

"She's too nervous," Dalton worried.

"Should we turn the sound down?" Phoebe wondered if the music could make a twitchy rat dangerously wild.

"Nah. Rowena likes music. Rats are very sociable," he said.

When the telephone rang, Phoebe hurried to answer it.

Iris sounded tired. "I just didn't want you to fret, sweetie. We'll be home in a while."

"Is everything okay?" Phoebe asked.

"Nothing of ours was damaged. It started in Wolf's area. Lia Wong had some tar and canvas delivered — she's painting with tar only now — and they left it in Wolf's part of the warehouse. While he was working on his sculpture with a blowtorch, he accidentally set fire to her tar and canvas. Everything of his and hers is ruined — a shambles. And of course Lia and Wolf are at each other's throats. We're bringing Wolf home with us."

"You're *what*?" Phoebe gasped.

"Dear, he has no place else to go. Who else would take him in? He's a rather difficult person."

"Mother, he *hates* children."

"Not so long as they're not around him. Now, he's very sensitive, so you will all have to be very quiet, and understand that he's been through a terrible ordeal."

"Mother, you're going to bring home a man named after a savage *beast*."

"Angel, he isn't *named* after a beast. He made up the name Wolf Chandon himself."

Upset as she was, Phoebe could not help being curious. "What's his real name?"

"We have no idea."

"Can't you take him to a hotel?" Phoebe persisted.

"Oh, love, he looks much too alarming. We'll be home soon."

There was one last hope. "If he's nervous, Mama, you might have a problem. Tiffany's cousin brought his rat with him."

There was silence on the telephone. Then Iris asked in a low, flat voice. "Brought his what?"

"His rat."

Iris spoke slowly, as if she were having trouble getting the words out. "What . . . is . . . it . . . doing?"

"Kind of running around."

Iris's voice sunk so low it almost vibrated. *"Running around where?"*

"In my room." It occurred to Phoebe that this might not have been a good time to mention Rowena. "But it's okay. She has a cage to sleep in."

"Phoebe." Iris Townsend's voice was low and steely. "You listen to me. You have that animal *in its cage* before we get home. Keep it in your room and out of sight. Wolf has a horror of rodents."

"Wouldn't it be easier to just send Wolf — "

Her mother hung up.

Phoebe went back to her room.

"What were you moaning about?" Tiffany turned down the boom box.

"My folks are bringing home this sculptor."

"Sculpture? Like a statue?" Heather looked interested.

"Sculptor." And I have yet to spring Amy on them, Phoebe thought. "He makes statues out of iron and he managed to set fire to the warehouse with his blowtorch."

"What warehouse?" Tiffany asked.

"Where my parents practice."

Dalton looked impressed. "They're into gymnastics?"

Phoebe was beginning to feel she'd already explained more than she really wanted to. "Where they practice their piano and violin."

"Why would you keep your piano and your violin in a warehouse if you practice on them?" Dalton rubbed noses with Rowena.

"They practice for hours at a time. The people downstairs would probably get sick of it."

"They're that bad?" Dalton asked.

To Phoebe's surprise, Tiffany said, "They can't be that bad. They play music for a living, don't they?"

"How big was the fire?" Heather asked Phoebe.

"Medium, I guess. They're bringing Wolf here to stay."

"*A wolf?*" Heather's eyes widened.

"Wolf Chandon, the sculptor. We have to keep the rat in its cage and out of sight."

Dalton looked worried. "Out of *my* sight?"

"We can keep her in my room. They'll probably put Wolf in the den."

"Den?" Tiffany looked impressed.

"The study," Phoebe translated.

"But that's where your TV is," Tiffany protested. "And there's this great special on monster movies tomorrow at three!"

"So tomorrow at three we'll go in and watch the special." Phoebe was beginning to understand how a parent might get grumpy, explaining everything.

"We'll have to get in there before Wolf or your folks start watching something else. Once parents get interested in a program, they can be stubborn." Tiffany picked up Phoebe's clock radio. "I'll set it for two-thirty, so we can have the TV staked out by three."

Dalton opened his backpack and took out a handful of Bubble Yum. "Want some?"

Sitting in her room listening to tapes and chewing gum, with Rowena showing no interest in attacking anybody and Heather and Tiffany barely squabbling, it occurred to Phoebe that being part of a big family must feel like this. With brothers and sisters, a person would always have somebody to play tapes and watch movies with. It might even be all right to have a quiet little brother like Dalton, one that shared bubble gum and was no trouble at all. He even had a pretty agreeable rat.

When she heard knocking at the front door, Phoebe hissed, "Put it in its cage!"

Heather and Tiffany followed Phoebe to the door and waited in silent anticipation.

"Who is it?" Phoebe called.

"Me. Amy."

"Oh, *guy*," Heather muttered in disgust while Phoebe undid the chain and the bolts.

Phoebe had a feeling she should have mentioned earlier that Amy was coming.

"What is *she* doing here?" Tiffany demanded. "Nobody said she'd be here."

"Come on in," Phoebe told Amy, half afraid that she might run after her brother and make him drive her home.

Stepping into the foyer, Amy looked wary and uncomfortable.

"Let me show you where to put your stuff," Phoebe said quickly.

Looking at Dalton, Amy suddenly brightened. "Oh, wow! Look at that face! Look at those great big beautiful shiny brown eyes!"

Startled, Phoebe turned. But Dalton's eyes were still blue.

"What a great rat!" Amy cried.

Dalton looked very pleased. "You want to hold her?"

At least two of us are going to treat Amy all right, Phoebe thought, leading the way to her room while Amy cuddled Rowena. Three, if you count the rat.

"You can have that bed," Phoebe told Amy.

Heather narrowed her eyes. "Who gets the other one?"

There was a knock at the front door.

"Get Rowena in her cage!" Phoebe commanded.

Again, Tiffany and Heather followed her to the door. Suddenly it occurred to Phoebe that the two of them had probably complained to their parents about the weekend's plans as strongly as she had. But the fire and Wolf Chandon had lent a whole new, scary, and exotic tone to this evening. Heather and Tiffany were looking nervous but intrigued and expectant. And Dalton was telling Amy all about burned iron sculptures and the wild, weird man named Wolf who made them.

"Open up, sweetheart." It was Iris.

As Phoebe opened the door, everyone behind her fell silent.

Looking sooty and exhausted, Brian and Iris stepped in, not even smiling for Phoebe and her guests.

Phoebe could see that Heather and Tiffany were impressed by what her parents must have been through.

Then Wolf entered.

Phoebe had seen him the few times her parents had brought her to the warehouse, but she'd never spoken to him. He'd always been muttering fiercely to himself, shooting great jets of flame at sheets of metal.

Tall and gaunt, wild-eyed, soaked and blackened, he stepped into the foyer. His torn jeans, ancient gray sweatshirt, and tattered Army surplus jacket were grimed and soggy, and his rundown boots squished as he moved. Bits of ash clung to his black beard, and his face and hands looked as if he'd been sweeping chimneys in a heavy rain. His long, black hair was tied back in a ponytail.

He was plainly even more frightful than Tiffany and Heather had feared and hoped. Behind them, Dalton, his eyes fixed on Wolf, blew an enormous pink gum bubble. Then, not even seeming to realize he'd done it, he sucked it back in with a long, damp slurping noise.

Wolf Chandon's left eyelid twitched, and for a second it looked as if he might turn and leave.

Brian put a hand on his shoulder. "Wolf, you know our daughter, Phoebe. These are her friends . . ."

Handing Brian two full paper sacks, Wolf lifted from the floor a great construction of twisted, tormented black iron with things that looked like beaks and wings and claws sticking out all over it.

"You'll want to get cleaned up and into something dry," Iris said.

Clutching the iron monster close to his chest, Wolf followed Brian toward the bathroom.

As soon as the men were out of earshot, Iris fixed the children with a stern gaze. "No one is to mention the rodent, is that clear? Wolf is not to know he's sharing our apartment with a rat.

He's unstrung enough as it is." She turned toward the kitchen.

"Wolf?" Amy whispered to Phoebe.

"He is so weird," Heather murmured delightedly. "Like a hippie — or a highwayman from the Middle Ages."

Tiffany looked at her in disdain. "They didn't have highwaymen in the Middle Ages. They had to have stagecoaches before they could have highwaymen."

"And highways," Amy put in. "They had to have highways."

Tiffany narrowed her eyes at Amy. "You are so *ignorant* . . ."

"Okay," Heather says. "So he looks like a hippie or a derelict."

Iris stuck her head out of the kitchen. "No, dear. He's a genius."

Phoebe drifted in to watch her mother fill the kettle. "How long is he staying?"

"I don't know. A few days, a few weeks." Iris opened a tin and peered into it.

"Weeks! Mother! He hates me!"

It had taken Wolf little time to establish himself in the study. Already, he had scattered papers and old scarves and pill bottles and pencil stubs on the coffee table. Sitting on top of the television was his knobby metal sculpture.

Tiffany walked over to the set.

"Don't touch that!" Wolf cried.

Tiffany turned, startled and insulted. "I'm just going to turn on — "

"Don't jostle my work!" he warned fiercely.

Edging closer to the set, Dalton glanced up at Wolf's sculpture. "What's it supposed to be?"

"The End of Being," Wolf growled through his teeth.

"What?" Now even Heather was interested.

Wolf closed his eyes and took a deep breath. Then, speaking as if he were trying to remain calm in the face of some savage hostile tribe, he declared, "It is called *The End of Being*. That is its name. You are not to touch it. You are not to come near it. You are not to breathe upon it!"

"Boy," Dalton growled, once safely in Phoebe's room. "I have to put Rowena in a cage, and that guy has that iron thing right on your television set!"

4

Brian had changed into a ratty sweater and corduroy pants, Iris into a caftan that resembled an unironed cotton Indian bedspread. She served tea in the kitchen, probably because the adults still smelled rather sooty.

Tiffany watched. "You don't have any soda?"

"No, dear." Iris was firm. "Carbonated beverages do ghastly things to your teeth. Do you take fructose or honey?"

Tiffany looked at Phoebe helplessly.

Elbows planted on the table, Wolf Chandon gazed bleakly at the wall as he drained his cup.

While Iris and Brian made dinner, Wolf returned to the study.

Phoebe watched her father open can after can, all with exotic labels, few of which were in English. Tiffany and Heather stood well out of the way, Amy behind them with Dalton.

With this many people for dinner in any other household, Phoebe thought, it would be almost like a family . . . an uncle in the study, kids hanging around. But what do I have? A father opening cans from The Far East Trading Company's close-out sale, a surly smoke-stained sculptor sulking in the study. . . .

Tiffany stared at the label on the can Brian had just opened. Eyes wide, she poked Phoebe. EDIBLE FUNGUS, the label read.

"That just means mushrooms," Phoebe told her wearily.

Heather did not seem reassured. She peered uneasily at every can Brian opened.

At dinner, Iris sat at the head of the big library table in what was a combination dining room and place to stack up scores and scores of music scores.

Tiffany gazed warily at the food on her plate, now and then poking at it just barely, as if to be polite, or to see if it moved.

Wolf ate silently but doggedly, his bleak stare fixed on his place mat.

Iris and Brian tried to comfort him. "The insurance will cover everything," Iris soothed.

"I let it lapse," Wolf muttered.

While Iris and Brian still tried to console Wolf, they seemed to be finding it more of an effort. And all the time, neither Heather nor Tiffany nor Dalton nor Amy said a word.

So much for a family dinner, Phoebe thought.

Dalton ate everything on his plate.

Even before Iris served the canned mango

strips and factory-reject Peak Frean biscuits for dessert, Wolf slouched back to the study.

Amy and Dalton helped Phoebe and her parents tidy the table and do the dishes, but nobody spoke.

"Could I have something for my rat?" Dalton asked.

Iris spooned a little rice onto a paper towel and added a mango strip.

"Do you have any peanut butter, so she gets some protein?" he added.

Iris opened a jar of cashew butter and put a dollop on the towel.

As they left the kitchen, Dalton murmured to Phoebe, "I've never been in anybody's house where they didn't have peanut butter."

"She's so polite." Amy watched Rowena nibble at the mango bit.

"Rats have naturally good manners." Dalton got more bubble gum out of his backpack, handed two lumps to Amy, and unwrapped one for himself. "We'd better leave her alone, though. I'd hate to have giants stare at me while I ate."

In the study, Tiffany turned the television on. "Oh, this is supposed to be a *horrible* movie!" she cried delightedly. "You have to be over seventeen to see it in a theater. Look at all the blood already!"

Popping bubble gum, Heather and Tiffany and Amy sat in front of the set. Settling himself next to Amy, Dalton blew the most enormous bubble Phoebe had ever seen.

BLAM! The bubble blew up, all over Dalton's face.

"Here. You can get it off with more gum." Amy handed him the glob she'd been chewing.

Wolf rushed out of the study.

It seemed to Phoebe like a stupid movie. A car exploded, a house behind it caught fire, and zombies kept tottering forward.

Iris strode into the room, followed by Brian and Wolf. Stepping to the set, she turned it off. "No, no, no, no, no! We do not watch mindless violence. Wolf, I'm sorry. Phoebe, you take your friends back to your room."

"Mother, what are we supposed to do?" Phoebe had never felt more persecuted. "You tell Tiffany and Heather and Dalton to come over here, and then you won't let us do anything!"

"All right." Brian was firm. "We'll do some switching around here. Wolf, you can have Phoebe's room, and the children can have the study. But there'll be no horror movies, and no loud noises in here."

As Wolf started gathering up his belongings, Iris drew Phoebe into the hall. "Take the rat cage into the living room while Wolf is busy, then bring it into the study once he's settled in your room."

Collecting everything she needed to take to the study, Phoebe felt grumpy and mistreated. If she had brothers and sisters, she thought, at least she wouldn't be permanently outnumbered.

"Boy!" Tiffany observed. "That old shaggy Wolf is really taking over around here."

Wolf made two trips from the study to Phoebe's room, carrying armloads of his belongings.

He left *The End of Being* on the television set, growling, "Stay clear of my sculpture!"

Smuggling Rowena into the study, it occurred to Phoebe that it would be interesting to let Wolf get a glimpse of her. But she had a feeling that the uproar, tempting as it would be, might be too much stress for the rat.

Iris came in. "Would you five like to play Scrabble?"

Phoebe shook her head.

"Anagrams?" Iris suggested. "Charades — quiet charades? Popcorn?"

Nobody answered.

She turned the television set on to a nature special, with the sound very low.

Phoebe knew Tiffany and Heather would tell their parents just what a miserable time they'd had, just how out of it the Townsend-Fanchons were.

At bedtime, Wolf spent almost an hour in the bathroom and left half an inch of water and a pile of sodden towels on the floor.

When Iris and Brian came into the study to open out the Hide-A-Bed, Brian gazed at Rowena as if she were a cobra. "There's no way it can get out of that cage?" he asked Dalton.

"Oh, no, sir." Dalton rolled his sleeping bag out on the floor. "Not unless I unlatched her door."

Phoebe had never been to a slumber party. She'd always imagined how much fun it would be, with everybody giggling and whispering late into the night.

There was no whispering now. There was no giggling. There was only Rowena running around and around on her squeaky exercise wheel. It struck Phoebe that it was cruel to keep anything in a cage. Nothing to do but run around and around on a wheel would drive any rat crazy.

If anybody in this room but Rowena and I is awake, Phoebe thought, it's somebody too depressed to make a sound.

SOUND!

The sound exploded the night — drums, guitars, bass, synthesizers.

"BUH-UH-UH BAYBEEEEEEEEEEEEE . . . UHHH!"

As Tiffany sat up with a shriek and Dalton yelped, Phoebe heard Wolf's terrified howl and saw her mother and father rush past the study, to her room.

The music stopped.

Stalking into the study, Iris switched on the

light and fixed Phoebe with an icy glare. "*Who set your clock radio for two-thirty* A.M. *on a rock-and-roll station?*"

Phoebe and Dalton and Tiffany stared at Iris silently.

"Is it morning?" Amy muttered groggily.

Heather only groaned.

With something between a snarl and a hiss and a sigh, Iris wheeled and tromped back to the master bedroom.

"How could you have set the clock radio for two-thirty in the morning?" Heather whispered at Tiffany.

Tiffany was even more touchy than in the daytime. "How was I supposed to know which was A.M. and which was P.M.? Mine says which is which."

"*Mine* has a red light for P.M.," Heather snapped. "Everybody ought to know that."

At breakfast, nobody spoke.

Phoebe and Tiffany were making up the Hide-A-Bed. Dalton, Heather, and Tiffany were rolling up sleeping bags when Wolf came into the study. "Did anybody see my sketch . . ." His eye fell on *The End of Being*.

"*What* . . ." Lurching across the room, he reached for the glistening pink glob on the end of one of *The End of Being*'s spiky tentacles.

"Oh. Sorry." Quickly, Dalton pulled the used bubble gum off the limb, leaving only a little pink on the tip.

Seizing the sculpture in his arms, Wolf staggered out of the room, so outraged he didn't even notice Rowena.

Minutes later, Brian came into the study, looking stern. "All right. Who stuck bubble gum on *The End of Being*?"

"I just put it there so I wouldn't lose it," Dalton explained. "It was hardly used at all."

Brian strode out of the study.

Phoebe could hear low, strained voices in the kitchen.

A few minutes later her father stuck his head into the study and motioned to her.

She followed him into the hall, where her mother stood.

"Tell your friend Jamie you will all be delighted to go to the fair." Iris sounded tense.

Phoebe was astonished, then wary. "She didn't invite any of them."

"It is not up to her to decide who goes." The veins in Iris's neck stood out, but her voice was still low. "Admission to the fair is not by invitation from your friend only. Anybody with the money can go to a county fair."

"But nobody brought money . . ."

"We will pay everybody's admission," Brian put

in. "We will give you each a small amount of money for admission and snacks and rides."

"But, Mama," Phoebe protested, "we can't afford it."

"We will find a way," Iris assured her. "If we have to eat sawdust for the next six weeks, we will find a way."

Yesterday, Phoebe realized, she would have been beside herself with the thrill of going to the fair. Yesterday there were no complications. Yesterday her parents weren't trying to force her to go. "What about Rowena?"

"She will be perfectly safe in her cage. Nobody will harass the rat, believe me."

Phoebe still felt uneasy. "I don't know how Dalton will feel about leaving her."

Brian took out his billfold.

"But what about no child of yours is going to take a public conveyance to San Mateo?" Phoebe asked.

Iris massaged her temples with her thumbs. "You and your friends will be perfectly safe together. I guarantee it. Five minutes in the vicinity of your . . . group, and any bus hijacker, any evildoer, any escaped criminal would turn himself in to anybody in a uniform, begging to be locked away. . . ." She held up her hands. "I'm sorry. I just think it would be . . . restful . . . if we all had a few hours . . . separated, adults from children."

Phoebe looked at her parents soberly. "How much are you going to give us?"

"My folks gave us each fifteen dollars to spend, and they're not coming with us."

Phoebe could see Tiffany and Heather absorbing that information. Amy, Phoebe knew, was simply relieved at the idea of not being cooped up with those two all day.

The only problem now would be to convince Dalton to leave Rowena.

"Fifteen dollars?" He seemed to be tempted. "What do they have at the fair?"

"Food, and stage shows, and rides, and animals," Amy told him.

"Scary rides," Tiffany put in. "Fairs always have junk food and scary rides."

"Hey!" Dalton got to his feet.

5

It is truly humiliating, Phoebe thought, to have your father ride the bus with you to the train station.

Once there, he bought their tickets, gave them each a timetable, and told them exactly what stop to look for.

"Oh, I've already . . ." Amy began, but Brian showed them on a map where to get off and where the fairgrounds were. Then, on everybody's timetable, he circled the train they were to take back and where to get it. He told them to leave early so they'd be sure not to miss it. He told them the spot where he would be standing to meet them when they returned. He made them promise they would all stay together, never go anywhere alone, speak to nobody but train conductors, police officers, people identifiable as fair employees, people who took food orders . . .

They all promised to obey all his advice and

commands. Then he saw them aboard and watched them leave.

Phoebe waited for somebody to say something about her father's performance.

"My dad," Amy confided, "does the exact same thing."

Phoebe had never been down the Peninsula before. She'd always imagined it would be green and hilly. Instead, all she saw from the window were fences and gray corrugated building fronts and billboards.

For the first half hour or so Dalton fretted. "I never should have left Rowena. She doesn't even know anybody at your house."

"I bet the fair will have rides so scary you almost throw up on them," Tiffany mused.

"Really?" Dalton breathed.

The fairgrounds seemed to stretch on for blocks. Hordes of people were going in and streaming out, some of them headed for the racetrack just a few hundred feet to the north.

When she got out of the car, Phoebe stood still a moment, watching the scarlet, green, and blue flags snapping over the gates.

Once through the gate, she stopped, just to make sure nobody she'd come with was missing.

They were in a midway swarming with people,

lined by booths and rides, with long, low buildings ahead and to both sides.

Phoebe sniffed. "Wow. It doesn't even smell like San Francisco."

"Well, your different fairs have different smells." Amy led the way toward a display board that had a map of the fair and a schedule of events. "You've got your basic smell of caramel popcorn, cotton candy, suntan lotion, Woolworth perfume, and wet diapers. Then, at the boardwalk at Santa Cruz you get the smell of the ocean thrown in . . . saltwater and seaweed. Then at smaller fairs inland, you get dust and more sweat. Okay. Stage show is at two. Pies and cakes and stuff are judged at one. What we should do is take in all the free stuff first so our money will last."

Dalton gazed at two little boys walking past with pink cotton candy. "Could we just get one of those first?"

"You don't want to get that stuff in your hair until we're ready to leave," Tiffany advised. "We should go on the scariest rides first. There's no sense eating anything before you make yourself sick to your stomach."

"Rides!" Dalton gazed over at a towering machine that was hurling people around in cages attached to long spidery arms. "Look! That one turns you all the way upside down! It could probably spin you right out of the fairgrounds if it wanted to!"

Phoebe was absolutely certain that she did not want to be whirled around and spun upside down. "I'm not going to spend a penny of my money making myself throw up."

"How about some of the free exhibits first?" Amy suggested.

"Exhibits?" Heather rolled her eyes in disgust. "I'm going on that ride."

"Amy and I want to start with free stuff," Phoebe said firmly.

"I'm going to hang out with Amy," Dalton announced.

"Okay. So take him." Tiffany nudged Dalton toward Phoebe. "He'd chicken out once we were in the air, anyway."

"No," Phoebe said. "I have the money, and we're all going to stick together. If I lose anybody, it would wreck the day."

"You know what's really neat?" Amy offered. "The Hall of Flowers."

"Flowers." Tiffany rolled her eyes in disgust.

To Phoebe's relief, though, nobody actually rebelled. She wasn't sure what she would have done, *could* have done, in that case, since she was still getting over the amazement that she stood up to Heather and Tiffany at all. Only the thought of explaining to everybody's parents how she'd lost any of the people with her had moved her to such a stand.

The Hall of Flowers was a big, low building, cool and misty and fragrant, full of little separate gardens, some of them with fountains and mossy paths. Even the people wandering around seemed calmer, less hurried than those outside on the midway. Dalton walked quietly between Phoebe and Amy.

There weren't many eight-year-old boys you could take through a flower exhibit, Phoebe thought. It wouldn't be at all bad to have a little brother like Dalton, somebody to look after, somebody to look up to you.

He looked up at Amy. "Do you go steady with anybody?"

"For Pete's sake!" Tiffany snorted. "She's not even eleven."

Dalton stopped before a small garden filled with tall, green spiky grasses and bright, waxy lilylike plants. "Wow! Just like those flowers that made everybody crazy in *Star Trek*." Stepping as close to the blossoms as he could get, Dalton inhaled deeply.

Dalton sniffled.

Dalton sneezed.

He sneezed again, and again, so violently that people turned to stare at him.

"This is embarrassing." Tiffany grabbed him

by the hand. "Let's get him out of here."

Once they were out of the Hall of Flowers, his sneezes slowed down. In the sunlight, Phoebe was alarmed to see just how bleary-eyed and foggy-looking he'd become in a matter of minutes.

"I could have told you!" Tiffany growled at Phoebe. "What a mess." She glowered at Dalton. "Did you remember to bring your allergy medicine?"

He shook his head.

"What do you mean 'You could have told me'?" Phoebe demanded. "Nobody told me he had allergies."

"I was supposed to bring his medical records?" Tiffany flared.

Dalton wiped his nose on his sleeve and sneezed again.

Phoebe wasn't sure whether bad allergies could give someone chills or fever, but she thought it was probably a good idea to get him out of the sun anyway. She nodded toward a big low building on their right. "That says Food Fair. We can probably get him something to drink in there."

"That's mainly food exhibits," Amy told her. "Home-baked cookies and breads and . . ."

Tiffany turned a hawklike gaze on her. "Free samples?"

"Sometimes," Amy said.

Taking Dalton by the hand again, Tiffany headed for the Food Fair building.

Phoebe couldn't help but feel sorry for him, so sneezy and miserable he didn't even object to being hauled around like a little kid.

The hall was buzzing with people, and the smell was a dizzying mix of pickled peaches, barbecue sauce, hickory smoke, nutmeg, mustard, cinnamon . . .

In the booths and at the tables, earnest fast-talking people demonstrated blenders and juicers and mixers and nonstick cookware.

Amy led the way past the bustle to a middle section of the building, and there were the kind of things Phoebe expected a county fair to have. One table was covered with jellies and jams and preserves in glass jars with hand-printed labels. On another table were nothing but cakes — fudge cakes, pound cakes, carrot cakes, upside-down cakes . . .

"Judging of the pies in ten minutes at Table Eighteen," came a voice over the loudspeaker, and the people in the hall started drifting toward a table with a pennant reading 18 over it.

"Pies! They must give them away after they judge them." Tiffany hurried toward the pennant.

"Why do you think so?" Phoebe had to trot to keep up with her.

Tiffany didn't slow down. "Well, they sure can't just throw them away, can they? You think everybody that bakes one wants to take it back after all the judges have eaten part of it? Or do you think they just let them sit there and rot?"

Table 18 was really four long narrow tables arranged in a square with a space in the center. In the space stood a woman in a coral-colored dress, a man in a blue suit, and a man in a gray plaid suit. Each wore a blue ribbon with JUDGE printed on it in gold.

Phoebe wondered how the judges got into that space. Had they crawled under the tables when nobody was looking? Had they stood there while the tables were put around them and all the pies put on the table? The pies were almost edge to edge . . . apricot, lemon cream, apple, pumpkin, blueberry, each with a number stuck on a little flag in its middle.

As people gathered closer, Phoebe's group was pressed to the very edge of the table bearing all the berry pies.

"Pie judging, Table Eighteen, beginning now with the berry pies," the announcer intoned over the speaker.

"Hey!" Tiffany looked as pleased as if she'd got everyone there by some great act of cleverness.

Dalton looked tired.

Holding paper plates and plastic forks, the three people in the middle of the square hovered over the table. Moving aside the number one, the woman judge eased the tip of a server into a boysenberry pie.

Dalton sneezed, a great, wet, wrenching sneeze.

As the people around him flinched, the woman dropped the server.

With her fork, she tried to fish it from the pie.

"Well, it's ruined. It's out of the running." The judge in blue looked grim.

"What do you mean?" demanded a gray-haired man standing beside Amy. "Disqualify my pie because some lump of a kid sneezed on it?"

"I'm not going to taste any pie that's covered with germs." The judge in blue was stern.

"No telling how far that sneeze carried . . ." The judge in the gray suit looked at Dalton, who was sniffling miserably. ". . . or what that kid has. Better cover everything in this section and dump it before the virus or whatever spreads."

The gray-haired man struggled toward Dalton.

"Who sent you, kid? Who sent you to wreck my pie? Was it Blakely?"

A man standing next to Phoebe shoved Dalton aside. "You're paranoid, Al, paranoid. You wouldn't know how to bake a winning pie if your own mother was coaching you."

A cloud of outrage and hostility spread around the berry pie bakers and onlookers. Nose to nose, they faced off. Some wanted all the pies disqualified, some were for eating them on the spot, and many wanted Dalton thrown out of the exhibit.

Al leaned over the table, his fists almost in the pies. "Paranoid? You pay a kid to sabotage me, Blakely, and you call me paranoid?"

Grabbing Dalton by the shoulders, Phoebe shoved him through the crowd of shouting, shoving adults.

As she reached the exit, uniformed guards passed her, running toward the commotion around Table 18.

Poor Dalton was shaken with sneezes, one no sooner done than another began. Phoebe did not dare slow down until they were halfway down the midway from the Food Fair.

Dalton's eyes and nose were red, and he looked weak and exhausted.

"There must be something we should do for him," Amy said. "I'd better call my mom."

"Nah. She'd make us leave," Heather objected. "Put him on a ride. Something awful enough might scare the sneezes out of him. It's supposed to work for hiccups."

"I think we should leave." Amy was solemn.

"What do you mean, leave?" Heather demanded.

"That was very hostile back there," Amy pronounced. "Those people turned into a mob."

Heather edged closer to Tiffany. "Is that Al coming toward us?"

Without even looking, Tiffany shoved Dalton

into the nearest building. LIVESTOCK EXHIBIT read the sign over the entrance.

Inside, the place smelled of manure and dander.

"Dalton," Phoebe asked, "are you allergic to fur or feathers or anything like that?"

"He has a rat, doesn't he?" Tiffany challenged. "Besides, he can't hurt cows or sheep by sneezing at them."

The building was not as crowded as the Food Fair, and far more peaceable, full of the soft grunts and lowing of pigs and calves.

In a small fenced area to their left, a girl was brushing a lamb. The animal stood quietly, calm and gentle, turning its head a little to watch her through lovely brown eyes.

"It's beautiful." Just looking at the lamb made Phoebe feel good.

Dalton sniffled. "My folks won't even let me have a dog."

"It's not a *pet,*" Tiffany said. "It's going to be lamb chops."

It took Dalton a moment to understand. Then his face got even more pale and his eyes more teary.

"Why did you have to tell him that?" Phoebe demanded.

"Hey. Look, Dalton," Amy said. "Over there."

"Exotic Edibles," Phoebe read. "Exotic means strange and unusual. Edibles means things to eat."

"We had enough strange and unusual things to eat at your . . ." Tiffany began, and then thought better of it.

"I bet they'll have great stuff like stuffed mushrooms and dried papaya and braised tofu!" Phoebe led the way toward the Exotic Edibles.

6

As Phoebe gazed at the snakes and lizards and bugs curling and stretching and scurrying around their cages and containers, a foul and clammy suspicion began to creep into her mind.

Dalton leaned on the rope separating him from a table with an aquarium full of frogs. "Aren't they neat?"

"Excuse me," Heather said to a man standing behind the table. "Where are the strange and unusual edibles?"

"All around you," he said.

"No," Amy said politely. "We mean the stuff to eat."

The man looked down at her. "That's right. Haven't you ever had frogs' legs?"

Dalton sneezed, a great shuddering explosion that sent him pitching into the rope. As the man grabbed for the left standard that held the rope, the right standard toppled.

Hands out in front of him, Dalton landed against the table so hard the aquarium rocked over on its side.

As frogs leaped out all over the table, the man dived to retrive them. "Get that kid out of here!"

Dalton was already running for the exit.

When Phoebe and the others caught up with him on the midway he was wide-eyed and sweaty, his right hand under his shirt.

"That was great!" Tiffany growled at him. "Keep it up, kid, and you'll get us thrown out of the fair!"

Phoebe could feel her own patience with Dalton dwindling, but she reminded herself that he couldn't help being allergic — and eight years old.

"I would just as soon leave." Dalton's voice was small and shaky.

"Like heck!" Tiffany told him. "We haven't even spent our money!"

"That's okay," he said. "I'd just as soon go."

"There's a stage show in five minutes," Amy said.

"I think we really need to get out of this place," Dalton insisted.

Heather bent until her face was close to his. "Look, kid. You have sneezed on exhibits, and fallen into exhibits, and generally been a natural disaster. Now, you are going to do what we decide. *What is that moving under your shirt?*"

"They were going to eat its legs!" he quavered.

"You!" Tiffany dragged him down a side lane, between a popcorn booth and a balloon stand.

"I won't give it back." Scared and sniffly as he was, Dalton was defiant, and determined.

Heather narrowed her eyes. "Listen, you . . ."

"Hey, I didn't see anybody else save a life in there," Amy said.

Heather turned to her. "Okay. Great. Then *you* give it back, because I'm sure not. We'll be lucky to get out of here before we're all arrested."

"What we'll do," Amy said, "is leave money at the gate to pay for the frog."

Phoebe wondered how soon the man would realize he was missing a frog, and start figuring out why. "But we don't leave our names or anything."

"We certainly don't," Amy said. "We just ask how much a frog would cost, and leave the money for its owner, with a note."

"Not a signed note," Phoebe said.

"Not a signed note," Amy assured her. "Dalton, keep the frog under your shirt, and let's get out of here."

His eyes bloodshot, his nose raw, Dalton gazed at her. "You are the most understanding person I ever met."

Once out of the fair, they looked around them.

"Hey!" Heather said. "We could go to the races!"

"Sure." Tiffany fixed her with a withering glance. "Take a frog to the races!"

"What we've got to do," Amy said, "is turn it free."

Dalton looked at her, stricken. "I can't . . ."

"Dalton," Amy told him, "you can't bring a frog on a train. You couldn't keep it under your shirt all the way to San Francisco. It would dry out, and probably die."

"You don't even know what it eats," Phoebe pointed out.

"Probably worms," he sniffled.

"Okay. That's it," Phoebe said. "The frog does not come home to my place."

"Besides," Amy told Dalton. "You couldn't let it run around the way Rowena does. And it's cruel to keep anything cooped up in a tank or a cage or a pen."

"So?" Heather challenged. "He should let it go, right here in the parking lot?"

Amy looked at her calmly. "We'll let it go in a pond, by Coyote Point."

It was a long walk to Coyote Point, especially with Dalton carrying a frog and sneezing all the way, and the rest of them braced for the moment it might get away from him.

They stopped at a gas station while Phoebe cadged a few wet towels to wrap the frog in.

Phoebe kept thinking of the cotton candy, the stage show, and all the wonders back at the fair, all the unspent money in her pocket.

But how could you be mad at a kid for saving a life?

Phoebe was sure she'd never walked this far before, even at camp. Heather and Tiffany were so short of breath they'd stopped fussing and just trudged on.

But Amy led them into a wild-looking area, all grass and bushes and weeds. Phoebe could not help thinking of snakes.

Dalton was sneezing so hard, Amy stopped. "Feeb, you stay with him. I'll take the frog."

"No," Dalton wheezed. "I want to see him off."

Phoebe was glad to sit with Heather and Tiffany in the weeds and let Dalton and Amy struggle through the bushes.

"She found a perfect, hidden pond, and he just jumped right in," Dalton announced when they returned, and looked up admiringly at Amy. "You really do know your way around here."

They got to the station with sixteen minutes to spare.

Sitting dusky and weed-clawed on the bench, Heather said, "Some fair."

"This is shaping up as the dumbest weekend I have ever spent." Tiffany scratched a bug bite on her ankle.

Even with all that money, Phoebe thought, I couldn't show anybody a good time. And now it's back to the apartment, not being allowed to do anything because of Wolf Chandon, and then over to Heather's, where she and Tiffany will treat the rest of us like . . . like frogs.

Brian was waiting for them at the San Francisco station.

"My." He greeted them. "You must have had an . . . active time at the fair."

"Could we stop somewhere and get something to eat?" Phoebe asked.

Brian looked at her. "You didn't eat at the fair?"

Phoebe shook her head.

"What did you do with all your money?" he pressed.

"Well . . ." Phoebe hesitated.

"Never mind," he said. "We have to rush home so you can get all your things together to go over to Heather's. You'll have dinner over there."

Iris, dressed in a long misty-gray gown, was in the foyer as they walked in.

"Get that rat over to Heather's while Wolf is out," she said.

"Can't he leave it here?" Heather asked.

"No." Iris was firm. "Wolf will be coming back to sleep. I certainly do not want him left alone with a rat."

It occurred to Phoebe that this might be a sure way to get Wolf out of their apartment, but she knew better than to say as much.

"I don't know how my mother's going to feel about this," Heather muttered darkly.

"Your mother will be in Monterey all night," Iris reminded her. "Now, you all pack up and hurry over there. We have to leave in a few minutes."

"I'm not sure about Chihuahua," Heather murmured darkly.

"Who's Chihuahua?" Dalton had stopped sneezing not long after they got on the train. Now he looked like some waif who has had a long illness and a pitiable life.

"My dog," Heather told him.

Dalton was not concerned. "Chihuahua . . . I've seen those little Mexican hairless dogs. They're pretty cute. Rowena could stand up to any of them."

"Excuse me." Grabbing Phoebe by the sleeve, Amy hauled her into the bathroom. "*We're* going to stay over at Heather's?"

Phoebe nodded.

"You didn't say anything about our staying overnight at Heather's," Amy persisted.

"Well . . ." I could tell her I just forgot, Phoebe thought. But that's lying. That's more serious than just not telling her something. "I thought if I did, you wouldn't come."

"You were right," Amy growled.

"But I really wanted you to. You're my best friend."

Amy did not soften. "You mean you thought two of us could stand up to two of them better than you could alone."

"That, too."

Somebody rapped on the bathroom door. "Is anything wrong in there?" Iris called.

"Yes!" Amy whispered savagely.

"When I asked you, it seemed like a good idea," Phoebe told her. "I thought if my parents got me into spending the weekend with Heather and Tiffany, I deserved to have somebody I liked."

Amy opened the bathroom door and walked out.

"May I use your telephone?" she asked Iris.

"In the kitchen, dear, but you must hurry." Iris looked rushed and distracted.

Phoebe did not dare follow Amy into the kitchen. Besides, she knew Amy would be calling home for somebody to come get her.

"I never knew your mother wore regular clothes, Feeble." Heather picked bubble gum off her slippers.

"My mother and father," Phoebe reminded her, "have a concert. They get dressed for it before they leave, in case the dressing rooms where they play are just bathrooms with people coming in and out. My mother says it destroys your mystique when half your audience has already seen you in the john."

"She seems eager to get rid of us," Tiffany observed.

A few minutes after Amy trudged back into the study, Iris hurried in. "Did you get whomever you called?" she asked Amy.

Amy shook her head. "I got our answering machine."

Brian strode in, wearing a tuxedo and black tie. "Now, you be sure to obey the Bowens' sitter. You're not to make any mess over there, or any racket. And you be quiet leaving here. Ms. Norberg still has laryngitis." Ms. Norberg rented the upstairs apartment.

"What's laryngitis?" Dalton wrapped his sweatshirt around Rowena's cage. "Can rats get it?"

"Laryngitis," Brian said, "means losing your voice. And I have no idea whether a rat can lose its voice."

"Will she ever be able to talk again?" Dalton asked.

"The rat?" Brian asked absently.

"Ms. Norberg," Phoebe said.

"Oh, yes. But she needs rest and quiet until she's up and around. Now, I want you all to be careful crossing to Heather's. You look both ways . . ."

"It's so in*sulting*," Tiffany observed, trudging across the street. "It's ridiculous."

"Well, he just wants to be sure we're safe." Phoebe felt obliged to defend her father, at least now and then.

Ignoring her, Tiffany fussed on. "A *sitter*. I'm old enough to *be* a sitter."

Heather was just as indignant. "We're probably the only twelve-year-olds in the city who have *sitters*." She glared at Phoebe. "It's because of *you*, I bet. I know Tiff and I could stay without a sitter if we didn't have ten-year-old trolls to look after."

"Two ten-year-olds and *him*." Tiffany scowled at Dalton.

"Don't you always have a sitter when your folks go out?" Phoebe asked.

"Yeah, but we're way too old," Tiffany sulked.

7

Mrs. Bowen, wearing a green knit dress and jade earrings, met them at the door.

"What have you been doing?" she greeted them. "You're all scratched up and dusty!"

Chihuahua came bounding into the foyer.

Dalton flattened himself against the wall, clutching Rowena's cage to his stomach.

With a great "gruuuumph!" Chihuahua reared up and planted his paws on Phoebe's shoulders.

She staggered, dropping her suitcase.

Chihuahua!" Mrs. Bowen chided as the dog licked Phoebe from forehead to neck.

"He's so . . . enthusiastic," Mrs. Bowen apologized, hauling on his collar. "Heather, you take your friends to your room. The sitter called to say she'd be a few minutes late. I took your casserole out of the oven. It's cooling on the counter, and your salads are in the fridge, so you can go ahead and eat right away. I left the number where we'll be." Her eyes fell on the covered cage. "Oh, dear.

I didn't know anyone was bringing a bird. Chihuahua, *down!*"

While Chihuahua dragged Mrs. Bowen after him, Amy and Phoebe followed Tiffany and Heather. Dalton walked bent over, protecting the cage.

Once in Heather's room, Dalton sat on one of the twin beds, clutching the covered cage to him.

"Heather," Mrs. Bowen said, "put Chihuahua out. It might make the bird nervous to be drooled on."

"Come on." Heather got hold of Chihuahua's collar.

Chihuahua rolled over on his back and went limp.

Setting her jaw, Heather dragged the dog down the hall, little rivulets of sweat running down her forehead and then her cheeks.

"That is no little Mexican hairless dog!" Dalton blurted once Mrs. Bowen had left the room.

"He's part mastiff and part Saint Bernard." Tiffany was already unpacking, laying her quilted pink robe on the bed.

Dalton was not soothed. "That dog could swallow the whole cage in one chomp!"

Heather came back, walking like a television wrestler who'd barely survived a grueling grudge match. "Chihuahua wouldn't hurt a fly."

Dalton hugged the cage tighter. "Sure, a fly could zoom away from him."

"Do you think you should tell your folks this is not a bird in the cage?" Phoebe wondered.

"Nah," Heather said. "No sense getting them all upset."

Dalton looked around him like a condemned prisoner seeking some escape. "How about we put the cage on the top shelf of the closet, with the closet door open and the bedroom door shut?"

"I can't reach it, and my mother doesn't allow me to stand on my furniture," Heather said.

Phoebe could see why. The furniture was all white, the chair with a blue chintz cushion, the bedspread and curtains white eyelet. Even the fluffy rug was white. It was not a room, Phoebe reflected, where you'd be comfortable standing on *anything*.

Heather's parents came back to her room.

Mr. Bowen was very solemn. "You kids remember . . ."

He recited almost the same warnings and cautions and directions that Brian had.

"Now, you come lock the door after us," he concluded. "Don't let anybody but the sitter in."

"Um . . . Amy's . . . a relative of Amy's will be coming to pick her up," Phoebe stammered.

"Nobody's coming for me," Amy told the floor. Her voice got even harder to hear as she looked at Phoebe. "If anybody in my family comes home at midnight, you think they'd want to turn around and drive to San Francisco and wake me up and everybody else? Besides . . . I don't even know Heather's address."

"So that's all settled," Mrs. Bowen said briskly. "Just be sure to wash up before you eat."

As soon as her parents were gone and the door was locked and chained and bolted, Heather turned to Tiffany. "Guy! You'd think they were going to Mars. So what do you want to do?"

"Eat," Dalton said.

"First let's see what's on TV." Tiffany went into the living room, Heather after her.

The telephone on the hall table rang.

"Get that, Feeble," Heather said.

"Go ahead," Amy told Phoebe.

Phoebe picked up the receiver.

It sounded like a carnival at the other end, with music and shouting and laughing.

"Um . . . hello?" Phoebe said.

"Oh, hi. This is Fauncine. I'm really sorry, but I can't make it. I suddenly came down with the flu."

"Just a minute." Phoebe put her hand over the mouthpiece. "Heather," she called. "I don't know who this is for."

"I can give you the names of some other sitters," Fauncine said, over the party noises.

Heather took the telephone from Phoebe. "Yeah? Oh, hi. Yeah? It must have come on pretty suddenly. No. No, that's okay. Never mind — we have a whole list of sitters."

"I could hear some *guy* telling her to get off the phone," she told Tiffany as she hung up. "Wait till my folks hear she stood us up for a *party*."

"So who are we going to get?" Phoebe asked.

"It's not my fault the sitter backed out at the last minute," Heather declared righteously. "It's not my responsibility. There's no sense my calling any other sitters anyway. They wouldn't come unless a parent asked them."

Tiffany nodded vigorously. "You know, once our parents find out Miss Boy Crazy didn't show up and we did just fine without her, maybe they'll see that we're a lot more responsible than some teenager."

"They'll feel *so* guilty for picking a sitter that finked out," Heather said. "They'll have to admit we're a heck of a lot better off by ourselves than with some dingbat. I mean, what if Fauncine had invited a bunch of boys over here?"

Phoebe felt a little nervous. Her parents, *everybody's* parents, had left thinking they'd have a sitter, Heather's sitter. On the other hand, she thought, Heather's right; no sitter would come to a house without being asked by an adult. It's not my problem, either. Here I am, dumped at Heather's against my will, without any sitter. Maybe after this certain people may think twice before they force their kid to go to anybody's house.

On the other hand, Amy's parents might never have let her come if they'd known she was spending Saturday night at some kid's house without any sitter.

"What are all those snuffling and gobbling noises?" Dalton asked Heather.

"Chihuahua! You dog!" Heather shrieked.

Chihuahua took his front paws off the kitchen counter, ears back, tail twitching.

"Look what you did!" Heather groaned.

The casserole dish on the counter was empty, licked clean.

The dog knew quite well what he'd done. Tail tucked between his legs, he ran from the kitchen and collapsed on his side in the hall.

"I thought you put him out," Tiffany said.

"I put him out in the kitchen," Heather confessed.

"You should have known . . ." Tiffany began.

Heather glared at her. "I know I should have known! But I haven't eaten since breakfast. I didn't even get a ride at the fair. I'm trying to contend with a rat. I have a dog who goes limp at important times so I have to drag him everywhere. I'm frazzled, okay?" She yanked open the refrigerator door. "Salads. Dumb green salads. And five teensy-weensy baked apples for dessert."

Tiffany scowled at the dog. "We're going to starve, and you scarfed down a casserole that would have fed a dozen of us."

Chihuahua whined.

"I'm already starved," Dalton quavered.

"Pizza," Tiffany exclaimed. "We can order pizza."

"With what?" Heather challenged.

"With the money we didn't spend at the fair," Tiffany told her triumphantly. "How much do we have, Feeb?"

"I left it at home," Phoebe said.

"What's that noise, like somebody choking?" Dalton asked.

Chihuahua had staggered from the hall into the living room to throw up on the Persian rug.

"Oh, poor baby!" Heather crooned. "Poor lamb!"

She led him to the back door.

The dog, Phoebe noted, was a pushover for smarm.

"Is Heather in trouble!" Tiffany murmured. "He's never allowed in the living room."

"We'd better clean that up," Amy advised. "Those rugs cost a fortune."

"So go get something to clean it with," Tiffany told her.

While Amy went down the hall, Phoebe and Tiffany scouted through the kitchen.

"They don't seem to have anything specifically labeled for dog barf on rugs," Phoebe ventured.

"We'll have to wait and ask Heather," Tiffany said.

In the parlor, Amy was scooping up what she could off the rug.

"That's my new bathrobe!" Tiffany yelled.

Amy shrugged. "You said to get something to clean it up with."

"You'd better shake it out somewhere," Phoebe advised.

Snatching her robe, Tiffany hurried toward the bathroom.

"Be careful," Amy called. "It has a lot in it."

Heather came in from the kitchen. "I left Chihuahua on the back porch in case he still feels — Oh, boy, does that smell!"

"Got any old rags?" Phoebe asked.

Everyone stood back while Heather worked on the mess, probably feeling, as Phoebe did, that the dog's owner should deal with the dog's little mistakes.

Then it occurred to Phoebe that they would all have to face Heather's parents in the morning.

"It still looks awful." Pale and queasy, Heather squatted on her heels.

Nobody could agree on what the next steps should be. They went back to the kitchen to think about it.

"Salt." Amy sounded certain. "Salt for the smell and lemon juice for the stain."

"Baking soda," Tiffany advised.

Phoebe thought hard. "How about dishwasher detergent?"

"Vinegar. Vinegar works for anything." Heather, being Heather, was not about to accept advice. She climbed on the counter and got a bottle from the cupboard.

"Wine vinegar?" Tiffany peered at the label.

"That's all we've got."

In the living room, Heather emptied the bottle on the spot, then scrubbed at the mess with an old rag, trying not to breathe.

"Yeccch." Tiffany grabbed her own throat. "That's worse!"

"It's also purple," Amy observed.

"Give me that salt. At least it will absorb the vinegar." Heather sat back on her haunches, holding her nose.

She emptied the box of salt on the rug.

"Now how do you get the salt up?" Dalton asked.

Heather looked up at him impatiently. "*Vacuum* it."

"Um . . . wet salt would short out the vacuum," Amy said. "It also might seriously kill you."

"So." Tiffany gazed down at the rug. "Now we've got a large, disgusting, salted smelly purple pile."

"If my folks come home and see that they'll kill me," Tiffany groaned. "Chihuahua is never allowed in the living room or the kitchen at mealtime."

"Baking soda will kill any kind of smell." Tiffany

thrust the box at Heather. "They even put it in deodorants — I've seen the ads on TV."

"Go ahead," Dalton said gently. "You can't make it any worse."

"So I was wrong." Dalton gazed at the caked baking soda as it rapidly turned wine vinegar violet.

Tiffany stared down at the mess solemnly. "It looks to me . . . if we can't vacuum it without getting electrocuted, it looks to me as if we're going to have to comb everything out of the fibers."

"I would use the lemon juice first," Amy put in, "to kind of break down the soda."

Horrible as the rug smelled and looked, Phoebe was almost grateful. Caught up in the challenge, Amy seemed to have forgotten that she hadn't wanted to come there.

"And maybe dishwasher detergent," Phoebe said. "That should clean anything."

After Heather poured lemon juice concentrate and dishwasher detergent on the salt-vinegar-soda rug spot, everyone watched the rug, appalled but fascinated.

"Look at it fizz!" Tiffany gasped.

Heather stepped back. "It's *hissing*!"

"You don't suppose it could boil over or explode or anything?" Amy whispered hoarsely.

"Maybe you should call your folks," Dalton told Heather.

She didn't take her eyes off the rug. "They aren't even there yet."

"Maybe we should . . ." Phoebe cleared her throat. "Maybe we should call the fire department."

"Oh, sure! Great!" Heather cried. "Fire trucks and sirens and all the neighborhood out on the street, maybe the police paging my parents in Monterey . . . that will be sure to convince my folks we didn't need a sitter!"

A dreadful but desperate possibility occurred to Phoebe. "We could ask Wolf."

"Wolf? Wolf Chandon?" Heather seemed close to breaking.

"He just had a fire," Phoebe pointed out. "And he works with a lot of weird materials. And he wouldn't be likely to tell your folks, because they'd never talk to anybody like him."

Heather was doubtful. "What about your folks?"

"Look, we'll just ask his advice about *a* situation. We don't have to say it's *your* situation."

"If I were you," Dalton told Heather, "I'd make up my mind. We'd better get out of here before this rug has some kind of chemical reaction you wouldn't believe!"

Still Heather hesitated. "What if Wolf isn't back from dinner yet?"

"Then we'll wait for him." Phoebe knew the only way to hurry Heather was to convince her.

"Why don't we just call over there?" Heather asked.

"Because Feeble has to go over anyway for the pizza money." Tiffany seemed to be coming to the end of her patience. "You wouldn't want to eat here, would you?"

"Not with the way it smells, to say nothing of what that carpet may do," Amy said.

Dalton gazed at the rug. "It's probably going to lie there and lurk and then blow up when we're ignoring it."

"I'm for getting out of here," Tiffany declared.

"Wait," Heather was obviously thinking of something vital. "Feeble doesn't have cable TV *or* a VCR. We won't have anything to do while we eat."

"Okay," Tiffany said reasonably. "We'll bring your VCR and some tapes."

"You get them," Heather said. "I'll leave a message for my folks that we have to go to Feeble's, just in case they call."

"Then if anybody calls here, they'll know your parents are out," Dalton observed.

Heather looked at him coldly. "I am *not* going to say 'Hi, parents, I am leaving the apartment empty and unguarded.' " She fiddled with the answering machine and then leaned close to it.

"Hi . . . uh . . . hi. If anybody is . . . if anybody is calling here for Heather, she'll be at Phoebe's number. And everything is fine. No problems at all. Um . . . we will call this number from Phoebe's number and leave a message so the people who own this number can hear it by remote."

"There." She hung up triumphantly. "Nobody but my parents have the code to play back messages that come in to this phone."

"That's a lie," Dalton said.

Heather glowered at him. "*What* is?"

Dalton was not intimidated. "Everything's not fine, and that rug and the smell are *problems*."

"That," Heather said triumphantly, "is why we're going to Feeble's for help, so that long before my folks get home everything will be fine, no problems."

"Okay," he said. "But I'm not leaving my sleeping bag here if that rug's going to explode."

"That is the dumbest thing I ever heard." Heather was plainly exasperated.

Quietly, Phoebe and Dalton and Tiffany collected their belongings. A little brother, Phoebe thought, might cause a certain amount of wear and tear on your nerves.

Outside the night was quiet, cool and damp, dark but for the corner lamps.

Heather held a leash with both hands while Chihuahua hauled her across the street. Dalton stayed several yards behind, with Rowena's cage wrapped in a sweatshirt and a pajama top.

Phoebe found the door key under the rock where her parents always left it.

Wolf was still gone.

"Let's order pizza before he gets here," Tiffany urged. "He looks like somebody who'd have no qualms about scarfing down a kid's pizza."

"How about Chinese food?" Phoebe suggested. "That way we can get everything vegetarian."

"Fortune cookies!" Dalton said. "Make sure they send fortune cookies!"

"Let me call my place and leave a message for my folks," Heather said.

She sounded more sincere on this phone than on the answering machine. "Hi, Mom, Dad. We're over here at Feeb . . . at Phoebe's just to get some important stuff, and everything's fine so you won't have to call back or anything."

Hanging up, she leveled a challenging stare at Dalton.

"Maybe we'd better put Chihuahua out." Phoebe wasn't sure the dog was quite finished throwing up.

Heather looked at her indignantly. "How would you like to be put out in the dark and the drizzle if you were sick to your stomach?"

Dalton sat on the floor, between Rowena's cage and Chihuahua.

"Okay. Feeb, I'll need a deep pan with a lid, and some kind of cooking oil and a big bowl."

Phoebe looked in the refrigerator. "How about rice bran oil?"

She heard Heather sigh.

"You guys set up the VCR while I make the popcorn." Amy turned on the stove. "Take the dog. I don't want him intercepting the popcorn before I get it in a bowl."

Phoebe decided she'd better go with the others to the study. She could trust Amy with a stove, but she was not sure she should trust Heather or Tiffany with her parents' television set.

Uneasily, she watched while they pulled the set out from the wall so that Heather could ease behind it.

Heather and Tiffany conferred tensely and fussed and argued as they plugged and unplugged wires and leads, while Dalton hovered over the cage and watched Chihuahua.

"Okay." Tiffany came to the front of the set. "That ought to do it. What tapes did you bring?"

"Stuff my folks don't even know I know they have. *Fright Night* and a couple of other gorier vampire movies." Heather helped Tiffany shove the television set back near the wall.

Phoebe had a feeling she didn't really want to watch anything horrifying while there were only kids and a dog and a rat with her. But she knew that if she said so, she'd let herself in for enough teasing to make a vampire movie seem tame.

"Where can I put Chihuahua?" Heather took her dog by the collar.

"You mean out?" Phoebe asked.

Heather looked like someone struggling to be patient with an impossibly dumb child. "I *mean* which room."

"I guess in here is as good as any. We can keep an eye on him." Phoebe could not help wondering how Wolf would feel about giant enthusiastic dogs with gurgling stomachs. She suspected Wolf might not be a dog person. On the other hand, it would certainly be interesting to see the man react when Chihuahua reared up and planted those paws on his shoulders.

"You think I'm going to let my dog watch *vampire* movies?" Heather was outraged.

"Oh, come on," Phoebe said. "You're telling me that dog would understand a movie?"

"How do you know what he understands?" Heather challenged. "Besides, if we all start screaming and gasping, it's just going to upset him. And if he gets upset, he might start throwing up again."

Phoebe thought her parents might be upset to learn that everybody who was supposed to be at Heather's with a sitter had come here. She was sure they would be deeply upset to come home and find their rug looking like the Bowens'. "Why don't we just go back to your place."

Heather looked at her in disgust. "Get real. You think I'm going to go back there with a rug that might go ballistic?"

"Besides," Dalton added, "nobody could eat over there. I bet the whole apartment smells of dog barf."

"And I'm sure not going to unhook this after I just got it all connected!" Heather squatted in front of the VCR.

"Okay. Vampire movie number one." Tiffany handed her a cassette.

"First let me set everything up," Heather said. "I think this is the right button — "

There was a scream from the kitchen.

Running in, Phoebe saw the yellow flames licking around the pan on the stove. She grabbed a dish towel before it occurred to her that setting a dish towel on fire, too, wouldn't help.

Heather grabbed Chihuahua by the collar and hauled him from the kitchen.

"Baking soda!" Amy yelled.

"Call 9-1-1!" Tiffany rushed to the telephone, through the oil and popcorn on the floor. She took a few skittering, sliding steps, and grabbed for the phone as if to steady herself. It was no use. Her right foot skidded to the left as her left foot kicked toward the ceiling, and she crashed on her back, holding the phone.

Phoebe opened two cupboard doors before she found a box of baking soda. Ripping the top off, she threw the soda toward the fire, only seconds before Tiffany, scrambling to her feet, grabbed a canister of whole wheat flour off the counter and emptied it in the direction of the stove.

But the flames had already sizzled out, leaving the stove, the floor, Amy, Tiffany, and the spilled popcorn covered with tan flour, oil, and baking soda.

It was a moment before anybody spoke.

"The oil just came spurting out of the bottle all over," Amy quavered.

"Don't you have a fire extinguisher?" Dalton asked Phoebe.

"Oh." Phoebe opened the cupboard under the sink. The red extinguisher was right in front of the detergents. "I guess, in the excitement, I forgot."

Dalton looked at Tiffany. "You know, the flour would have just exploded into more fire. You never put flour on a fire."

"I probably broke my back!" she flared.

"You couldn't stand up with a broken back." Dalton was not moved. "If you think somebody has a broken back, you never try to move them. You ask them to wiggle their toes."

"You ask somebody with a fractured spine to wriggle her toes?" Tiffany was torn between outrage and incredulity.

"That's what you ask them. Baking soda," he went on, "works on oil fires. Which is lucky." He gazed at Amy sternly. "But you never, *never*, fry anything when your parents aren't right there. And not even *parents* put a lot of grease in anything but a deep fat fryer." He shook his head. "Don't you guys learn *anything* at school?"

When nobody answered him, he said. "You'd better clean up the mess." He looked at Amy again. "Starting with you."

I don't know, Phoebe thought. I think the kid was easier to take when he was sneezing and frog-napping. Still, she knew he was right.

"You'd better go wash up," she told Amy.

"Not before she vacuums herself," Dalton said solemnly. "Or else she'll be a big glob of paste."

Heather stood with her back against the wall while Phoebe got the vacuum out of the hall closet.

"I never saw a person vacuum herself before," Heather observed.

When she'd finished, Amy turned off the vacuum and dragged it to the kitchen.

"I don't think so." Dalton stepped between her and the stove. "I'm not sure what all that flour and oil and soda and popcorn kernels will do to the motor. Better scrape up all you can and put it in the trash. Then you'll have to soak up all the grease with newspaper or paper towels." He turned to Phoebe. "I hope you have recycled towels."

This kid was so right, Phoebe thought, he ought to be put in a think thank. Permanently. "I'm sure they're recycled," she said, figuring that her parents would never be so irresponsible as to buy anything else.

"While you're cleaning the stove with detergent, you should soak the pot in hot water and soda, to loosen the burned-on grease," he advised. "After that you can scrub the pot and mop the floor with hot water and detergent."

"Oh. Here's your phone." Tiffany handed it to Phoebe. "It kind of came apart when I fell."

Heather surveyed the kitchen. "So do you have crackers or anything? If I don't eat first, I'll never be able to tackle this mess. Although I really shouldn't have to, since I didn't make any of it."

Phoebe felt weak and empty herself. Looking around her, she, too, felt a deep reluctance to start what was going to be another long, hard, depressing cleanup. Maybe Heather's right, she thought. Maybe food will give us the energy to dive right in and get the job done.

There were stone-ground whole wheat crackers in a cupboard, along with a round of soy cheese and six cans of passion-fruit nectar.

"We might as well see a movie while we eat.

Then we'll feel able to face the kitchen." Tiffany took the crackers and started for the study.

"We can't watch a movie! Wolf will be coming back!" Phoebe went after her.

"Just for a few minutes, while we eat." Heather inserted a cassette and pressed a button.

8

Phoebe knew they should all get to work. But just *thinking* of what they faced in the kitchen made her tired. Besides, she reminded herself, Wolf will have eaten already. When he sees the five of us in the study, he'll bolt for my room. We'll have to ask him about the Bowens' rug before he barricades himself in there.

"Scary music." Dalton leaned forward, watching the screen.

Everyone but Phoebe ate and drank slowly, eyes fixed on the movie.

I'll give it another minute, Phoebe thought, and then I'll just announce that we have five minutes to finish eating. We can watch the rest of the movie after the kitchen's clean.

As the vampire sunk his fangs into a girl's throat, Dalton set down his can of nectar. "Okay. How about we clean up the kitchen?"

"Not now!" Heather rasped as Tiffany shushed Dalton.

By the time the first victim had become a vampire, Phoebe was very sure that she was never going to watch another horror movie, and certainly not while she was eating or drinking.

"Well." She stood, trying to sound brisk and confident. "Time to get in there and tidy the old kitchen."

Suddenly, a thumping noise seemed to shake the apartment.

Thudd . . . thudd . . . thudd . . .

Dalton scrambled off the floor and onto the sofa between Amy and Tiffany. Then he clambered off and curled himself around Rowena's cage. Phoebe grabbed Amy's hand. Phoebe grabbed Tiffany's hand.

Dalton opened three pieces of bubble gum and stuck them all in his mouth.

Something, somewhere, somewhere in the apartment, howled, a long, low, eerie howl like that of some inhuman, haunted creature.

Tiffany made a small, strangled squeak in her throat, but nobody moved, nobody so much as let a long breath out.

Thudd . . . thudd . . . thudd . . .

The thuds came faster. The howls grew longer, starting low as a lion's moan and rising to an unearthly, shrill crescendo.

And they were coming from somewhere in the apartment.

Then came a sound of something clawing, like great talons ripping across wood.

Even if she had been able to move, to run, Phoebe would have been terrified to break from the group. Any motion would surely attract the attention of . . . whatever it was.

Phoebe closed her eyes and tried to put herself back at the Bowens' an hour ago.

The howling, the thumping, the clawing went on. When Wolf comes home, Phoebe thought wildly, and finds all our bodies . . . or finds us all gone . . . how will he explain that mess in the kitchen to my parents?

A long howl rose, and rose, and ended in a bark.

This was no monster's bark. This was the "come let me in" bark of a large, lonely, not terribly bright dog.

"Chihuahua!" Heather cried.

As she rushed from the room, Phoebe followed. No beast, no monster, no creature from the depths, would tangle with a beast as large as Chihuahua, a beast with inch-long fangs. And if the thumps and howls were from some unearthly creature, the dog would sense it — the dog would be barking in a frenzy, not yapping for somebody to come.

As Heather reached the door of Phoebe's room,

the barks became whines and snuffles, and the clawing even more vigorous.

Heather opened the door.

Thudd . . . thudd . . . thudd . . . THUDD . . .

Chihuahua wept like a dog that's been rescued from months of solitude. His tail wagged delightedly, thumping against Phoebe's dresser.

"Oh, no," Phoebe groaned.

Chihuahua had been busy. Even with his howling and wagging and clawing great deep grooves down the inside of Phoebe's door, he had made time to trash the room. Tiny, tiny bits of pillow were scattered all over the rug — the edge of which had been chewed into a slobbery mess. Half a dozen books lay strewn on the floor, soggy with dog spit. *The End of Being* lay in pieces, dripping.

Phoebe turned on Heather. "I thought he was housebroken!"

"He is," Heather retorted indignantly. "But this isn't his house. Besides, all the howling and clawing was to tell us he had to go out. It's not *his* fault if everybody panicked."

"So let him out now," Phoebe said through her teeth.

"I don't think he has to go anymore," Heather said, as Chihuahua reared up to lick her face.

"Heather," Phoebe growled. "Heather, in that case I'm shutting you in here with him until you clean up every bit of — "

Looking past her, Heather screamed.

"Oh, come *on*," Phoebe was disgusted. "That's not going to get you out of it."

But Chihuahua turned, staring at the window, his hackles rising and a low growl vibrating in his throat.

As Chihuahua's growl rose to a roar, Phoebe followed his gaze.

Peering in her bedroom window was a hideous, stark-white face, a face the color of no human countenance — no living human countenance.

Phoebe felt a hand on her arm pulling her from the room.

One hand clutching Phoebe's sleeve, the other Chihuahua's collar, Heather ran with them to the study.

"Vam . . . vam . . ." Heather's voice was like air escaping from a balloon.

"Kit . . . chen." Freeing her arm from Heather's grip, Phoebe dashed for the kitchen.

In a panicked rush, the others crowded after her.

One thing about Chihuahua — he did not sense fear. With no face at a window, he seemed to be more ready for a romp than a crisis. Pulling loose from Heather's grasp, he bounded into the mess of flour, soda, and grease on the floor. Grinning, tongue lolling, he rolled on his back.

Phoebe picked up the pieces of telephone and tried to fit them together.

"It's no use," Heather croaked. "We're trapped like rats in a cage."

Phoebe knew she was right. The thing was probably waiting for them to run out into the night, where it would pick them off one by one, or even two by two.

"Garlic!" Amy rasped. "Vampires and those things hate garlic!"

Phoebe had never thought about the likes and dislikes of vampires. She had no idea who "those things" were, but she didn't stop to ask. Frantically, she rummaged through the cupboards.

"What's this? What's this? What's this?" Amy reached past her and seized a small tin.

"That's not garlic!" Phoebe went on searching. "It's brown."

Amy peered at the label. "Seasoning Salt." She opened the container and smelled the contents. "It may have garlic in it."

"AAAAAGGGGHHHH!" Tiffany flattened herself against the refrigerator.

The white, unearthly face was at the kitchen window now. In the fog, it seemed to float above a white gown that flowed from its neck.

A hand, a pink hand, a hand that could not belong to that stark face, rapped on the pane.

Amy flung seasoning salt at the window, then fled with the rest to the study, where the draperies were pulled shut.

As they huddled with the dog, Heather slapped

a hand over Amy's face. *"Don't scream!* If we don't make a sound it will have to search for us!"

Amy pulled her hand away. *"Who's screaming?"*

"That's what it wants!" Heather whispered. "It feeds on terror."

Phoebe had to swallow twice before she could speak. "But if we yell, maybe somebody will hear us."

"On a Saturday night?" Tiffany challenged. "On a Saturday night in the city, *everybody's* screaming. Oh, guy . . . it's still tapping the window!" She clapped her hand over her own mouth.

Amy threw the last of the seasoning salt in sweeping arcs around them all, even Rowena and the dog.

Phoebe could feel her heart pounding like a Ping-Pong ball, and her throat felt as dry as if it were lined with felt. She sat on the floor, terrified to move, expecting the thing to come crashing through any window.

"Please! Please! Please!" came a thin, unearthly voice from outside the kitchen. The raps on the kitchen window were faster, now.

"What if it's the vampire's *victim*?" Dalton whispered.

"Oh, please! Please!" The voice seemed to fade, as if it were being drawn inexorably into some moldering grave.

"It's a trick," Tiffany muttered. "It's trying to throw us off guard."

The voice was gone, suddenly.

Outside there were only the sounds of singing, quarreling, fellowship from blocks away.

"It's only lulling us." Heather hugged Chihuahua closer.

"To take us off guard," Tiffany whispered.

Suddenly, Amy grabbed Phoebe's arm hard. "Footsteps!"

The footsteps were heavy, measured, deliberate.

The footsteps were right outside the front door.

"D . . . door's locked," Phoebe quavered, to reassure herself as much as anyone.

"That won't stop it," Tiffany murmured bleakly.

"What's it doing out there?" Phoebe whispered.

The footsteps stopped. There was a metallic sound.

Phoebe heard the door open.

A pale yellow wash from the street lapped the Berber rug on the foyer floor, and was gone as the front door closed again.

The footsteps, heavy, unhurried, came toward the study. In the dimness of the room, Phoebe groped for a lamp. Better see what stalked them than be wiped out like rats in a cage, anyway.

She found the switch. As she turned the light on, she heard Amy yell, "Begone, foul spirit!"

"Oh . . . Wolf," Phoebe said.

"Oh! Oooh!" Wolf Chandon pressed both hands to his chest. "You nearly scared the life out of me!" He sat heavily in a chair.

Even dizzy with relief as she was, Phoebe looked at Amy. "*Begone, foul spirit?*"

The knock was loud and heavy, at the front door.

Heather buried her face in Chihuahua's neck.

"Oh, please!" The voice was thin and reedy. "Please! It's Flo Norberg and I'm out here in my nightgown!"

"Who," Wolf demanded, "is that?"

Dalton scrambled into Wolf's lap. "A vampire!"

Phoebe had never been so shaken, so torn, so confused. What if it *was* Ms. Norberg out there in her nightgown in the cold and the fog when she was just getting over laryngitis? What if she got pneumonia and died because they didn't let her in? What if she came back to *haunt* whoever left her out there? Even if she didn't, how could anybody live with the guilt? Especially when they were all supposed to be at Heather's with a sitter.

"They can pretend to be anybody." Tiffany's voice was hoarse. "It's saying it's somebody you know just to lure you to the door."

"I know you're in there." The voice outside was piteous enough to melt the heart of anybody who didn't know anything about vampires. "It's Flo

Norberg, from upstairs. Please . . . please . . . I can't walk to a phone booth like this."

"Oh, for heaven's sake!" Standing, Wolf Chandon set Dalton down and strode into the foyer.

"Don't! Don't!" Tiffany cried.

Phoebe grabbed Amy. "Everybody — everybody — stay together!"

There was no need to warn them. They huddled as close as they could, ignoring the dog's licking and pawing at them.

They heard the front door open.

"Oh, thank you! Th . . . Oh." It was the voice that claimed to be Ms. Norberg's.

Wolf Chandon came backing into the study, speechless, pale.

After him came . . . it, that shocking chalky face, that white gown . . . white-and-red striped flannel gown, Phoebe noted.

With no idea that she could still make a sound, she croaked, "Ms. Norberg . . . are you alive?"

"Barely." The voice was strained and reedy. "I've been out there for I don't know how long begging you to let me in."

You may find a vampire masquerading as something else, Phoebe thought, but no self-respecting vampire was going to go around shivering and hugging itself in a washed-out red-and-white-striped knee-length nightgown and pink fuzzy slippers covered in lint. Vampires did not go for comedy.

On the other hand, there was that *face*. Even Wolf had backed against a wall and stood stricken.

Phoebe held on tight to Chihuahua's leg. "Ms. Norberg, I don't want to be rude, but you look . . ."

"It has dried. It has dried." The creature slapped its own cheek. "You're supposed to rinse it off after twenty minutes."

Phoebe shut her eyes. She'd not been prepared for anything this bizarre, even from a vampire. Did this creature want to come in because it had to rinse its face off?

"Oh." Wolf still kept his distance, but he found his voice. "You're wearing a . . ."

"A clay beauty mask." The voice seemed feeble as much with embarrassment as laryngitis. "It was drying when I heard this howling. I looked all through my apartment and then I went outside to see where it was coming from, and the door shut behind me. I kept tapping on your back windows, but finally I had to come around to the front door. And I had hoped nobody would see me looking like this." She stiffened. "There! There it is! The howling!"

The excitement, the weight of clinging children was too much. Howling, Chihuahua scrambled out from under them.

He bounded to that nightgowned apparition. He rose up on his hind legs and licked that ghastly, ghastly face.

"Oh, help!" the creature cried.

"Somebody get that mutt off the lady!" Wolf commanded, but he made no move to approach the dog.

With two great slurps, Chihuahua licked both sides of the visitor's face, leaving pink skin where he'd washed off the white. Then, with a great *thump* he leaned against her like a cat.

If you can't trust a dog, Phoebe thought, what can you trust?

The sight of human skin on the being's face seemed to jolt Wolf. Abashed, he asked, "Would you . . . would you like to wash your face?"

What seemed to be Flo Norberg said, "Oh, I would."

"Bathroom's at the end of the hall," he said. "How about something hot to drink? Warm you up."

"That would be wonderful." Then, glancing at Phoebe, the creature asked, "You wouldn't have a bathrobe or anything? I feel so . . ."

"Hanging on the bathroom door." Phoebe turned to her guests. "It's . . . it's okay."

Dogs did not go around kissing vampires — or following them to the bathroom.

She heard a roar from the kitchen. *"What happened in here?"*

9

"A casserole?" Wolf Chandon stood in the middle of the kitchen, surveying the mess. "This all started because the dog ate a *casserole*?"

"And threw up." Heather moved a little closer to Tiffany, as Flo Norberg came into the room.

Ms. Norberg's hair was damp, but her face was quite human, though she looked to Phoebe like a person who had been through a lot.

Flo had tied Brian's terry cloth bathrobe around her. As Wolf glanced at her, her face got pinker. Then she looked around the kitchen. "Oh, my."

Phoebe explained again about the dog throwing up on the Bowens' rug and their coming over here for help, and trying to make popcorn. She didn't mention Chihuahua trashing her room. There was no sense burdening people with too much information all at once. Better bring it up just before Wolf had a chance to see it.

Ms. Norberg drew the robe tighter around her. "The only thing to do is dive right in and clean this up so you can go back to where your parents think you are. Phoebe, if you have my spare key, I'll go up and change into jeans."

"Spare key?" Phoebe asked.

"You know. I gave your mother my extra door key for just this kind of emergency."

"Oh, yeah." Phoebe remembered now. "She keeps it on a big ring with all her own keys."

Flo brightened. "So where is it?"

"She took it with her."

Flo Norberg had class, Phoebe thought. She did not observe that this was a remarkably useless thing for Iris to do. "Okay. Where do you keep the cleaning supplies?"

Ms. Norberg passed out rags and brushes, buckets and mops. "You'll have to take the dog out of here and wipe the grease and flour and soda and . . . what is that sandy stuff on top of everything else on him?"

"Seasoning salt," Phoebe confessed.

"Wipe it all off his paws. We don't want to spread the mess any more than you did already. And then . . . I don't know. The best thing would be to give him a bath, but he's just a little bit large for that. Just blot him as best you can and then maybe comb him very, very thoroughly, *and do not let him near any furniture*!"

She gave everyone assignments. This woman, Phoebe thought, was a lot more authoritative than she'd looked in clay mask and flannel nightgown.

Even Wolf scrubbed.

Only Heather objected. "How come Dalton gets out of this?"

"He'd be telling us everything we were doing wrong," Amy said, "and he's had a hard day. He's still all pale and sniffly. Besides, it sounds as if he's busy straightening things up in the study."

"Besides," Tiffany said, "he is one weird kid. Don't you hear him in there muttering and whistling?"

"All right." At last, Flo Norberg stepped back to study the kitchen.

"It's never been this clean before," Phoebe allowed.

"And it's after eleven," Wolf growled. "I, for one, am going to watch the news and go to bed."

Dalton stepped into the kitchen. "Is . . . everything normal in here?"

"Better than normal," Phoebe told him.

He stepped back into the hall.

"But what about *my* rug?" Heather demanded.

"Your rug," Wolf told her, "is your problem." And he stalked from the room.

"Don't worry too much," Flo said. "The rug can't explode or dissolve. It'll just sit there, reeking."

The cry from the study sounded like an animal in pain.

Wolf Chandon stormed into the kitchen, holding pieces from *The End of Being*. "Who . . . who . . . *who* . . ."

Wolf Chandon plainly had not been around children for a long, long time. It was kind of sad, Phoebe thought. You could tell he *wanted* to swear and throw things and make gruesome threats, but he was too intimidated by a bunch of kids and their neighbor standing so still, listening to him sputter and rage.

Finally, he whirled and strode back to the study.

A few minutes later, Phoebe glimpsed him stomping off toward her room with the parts of *The End of Being*.

"What a disposition!" Tiffany muttered.

"Oh, wait!" Phoebe called out, but of course he didn't.

He was back in almost no time, charging into the kitchen, still carrying the parts of *The End of Being*. "That dog, that drooling, demented, demonic *monster* is in my room, destroying the premises!"

Phoebe resisted the urge to remind Wolf that it was *her* room.

"Since he'd already wrecked it, I figured I might as well put him in there," Heather told her.

"Wrecked it?" Wolf seemed to be teetering on the edge of a monumental tantrum. "He trashed it, destroyed it . . ."

"You kids get in there and clean it up," Ms. Norberg said. "And how about a cup of tea, Mr. . . ."

"Cubby," he said. "W . . . Will Cubby."

Heather barely muffled a snort.

Phoebe ignored a jab in the ribs from Tiffany.

Ms. Norberg turned a burner on. "Collect all the trash baskets you have. Put everything you can salvage into a clothes hamper and everything you can't into the baskets," she told the girls.

"Cubby!" Tiffany chortled as they walked into Phoebe's room. "Will Cubby. Wilber, Wilford, Wilberforce?"

"Dalton!" Heather cried. "What are you doing to my dog?"

Dalton let go of Chihuahua's jaws. "Just . . . looking in his mouth." And he fled.

"I don't suppose I could put Chihuahua in your parents' room?" Heather asked Phoebe.

"No. Definitely no. Absolutely not. You keep him on a leash, and you keep him in sight!" As Phoebe looked around her room, she felt very, very tired. The dog had attacked even more things this time around. The only comfort was that most of them were Wolf's.

"Wilber Cubby." Amy picked up pages of a book. "We could call him Willie."

Phoebe stood straight at last. Her back ached, but her room had never been so neat. Of course, she was throwing out a lot of her belongings, and Wolf's . . . Willie's.

She shoved her clothes hamper into her closet. One A.M. was no time to worry about *how* to repair anything.

As she and Amy and Heather and Tiffany trudged toward the kitchen with teeming wastebaskets, Phoebe noticed Dalton on his hands and knees in the parlor. "Don't you dare make a mess in there!" she yelled.

He didn't look up.

"You don't suppose the kid could be having a breakdown from all the scares tonight?" Amy looked worried.

"Nah," Tiffany reassured her. "It's just eight-year-itis. All boys that age are crazy."

Wolf was sitting at the kitchen table with Flo Norberg. "The point is," he was saying, "that the artist who wants to be understood is compromising himself right away."

Phoebe edged toward the back door, thinking it would be just as well if he didn't see how much of what he owned was now rubbish.

Flo stood. "Let's take the dog out while we empty the trash. Then everybody can get some rest."

"Dalton!" Phoebe cried. "We're going outside for a minute."

"No!" Dalton dashed into the kitchen. "No! Don't open the door!"

"Dalton, don't be dumb." Heather led Chihuahua onto the back stoop. "There's no vampire."

Still Dalton would not come out, only shut the door quickly after them.

Cradling *The End of Being* as if it were a spiky child, Wolf Chandon was so intent on explaining to Flo how an artist must endure any hardship that he didn't even glance at what was being dumped in the big trash cans.

After Chihuahua hauled Heather to a street lamp and back, Flo Norberg said, "Now, everybody is exhausted, so I suggest we all get some rest."

She helped Phoebe pull out the Hide-A-Bed sofa in the study. "If we were pioneers, we could squeeze six or seven kids on that." She was bleary-eyed but agreeable. "You girls take that, and I'll take one sleeping bag and . . . where's the little boy?"

"Dalton!" Tiffany called sharply. "You get in here and get to bed!"

Wolf came out of Phoebe's room. "There are no pillows."

"The dog ate them." He takes over my room, she told herself, and he gets the pillows that are . . . were . . . in my room. A deal's a deal, even if nobody spelled out the details.

"Dalton!" Tiffany bellowed.

Wolf withdrew, shutting Phoebe's door hard.

Dalton came straggling into the study.

"You snuggle into your sleeping bag and settle down," Flo told him.

"I . . . I can't."

Flo was patient. "You may feel wide-awake now, but that's only because you're so over-tired."

Dalton sniffled.

"Do you have anything for that cold?" Flo asked him.

"It's not . . ." Dalton's words were cut off by great, shuddering sobs. "It's . . ."

From Phoebe's room came a shriek so hideous, so harrowing, so shocking that she felt it to the marrow of her bones.

It's not over! It seemed to her unspeakably cruel that after all they'd gone through, as soon as they dared relax, some new and even more ghastly horror was upon them.

Wolf Chandon staggered into the study, making frightful, strangled, gurgling animal noises in his throat. With shaking hand, he pointed toward Phoebe's room. "Alive! Alive!"

"Oh, boy!" Dalton dashed past him into the bedroom, then stood peering around him.

"Bed," Wolf croaked. "In the bed . . ."

The covers of Phoebe's bed were all tumbled, as if someone had thrown them aside to leap out.

Dalton threw the covers back all the way to the foot of the bed.

"Awwwww," Amy and Tiffany crooned.

"Don't tell me what it is unless somebody has to kill it," Flo quavered.

"Get Chihuahua out of here!" Phoebe commanded.

Heather hauled the dog from the room.

"Rat babies!" Phoebe murmured.

Flo shut her eyes. "I asked you not to tell me."

"That's why she's been edgy!" Dalton looked accusingly at Wolf. "She found a cozy, private place to have her babies, under the sheets at the foot of the bed, and then you had to come barging in!"

Crouched with his back against a wall, Wolf ran trembling hands through his hair.

Phoebe almost felt sorry for the man. "He didn't hurt them, Dalton." She gazed down at Rowena, who was busily washing the six tiny ratlets around her.

"Aren't they adorable?" Amy murmured.

Wolf stumbled to his feet and lurched toward the bathroom.

"But how did she get out of her cage?" Phoebe wondered.

"I let her out," Dalton said.

"Why?" Tiffany demanded in astonishment.

"When the vampire was coming," Dalton explained. "I let Rowena out so she wouldn't be trapped like a rat. Then I couldn't find her, and I was afraid if I said anything that Wolf would set out traps or something."

Flo's voice was hoarse. "Phoebe, you're absolutely sure your mother took my key?"

"Oh, yes," Phoebe said.

"All right. All right." Flo hugged Brian's robe around her, and began talking to herself. "It is cold. It is foggy. It is two in the morning. *I have no place to go.*" Closing her eyes again, she said, *"Count the rats."*

They obeyed. "Rowena and six babies," Phoebe reported.

"Once more."

She made them count three times, and each time the total was the same.

"Bring the cage to their bed," Flo said.

Dalton obeyed.

"Now. Very, very carefully, put *all* the rats in the cage."

"She needs more bedding for them," Dalton said.

"Fine. Fine." Flo's voice trembled only slightly. "Put something nice and soft in the cage, and hurry."

"I've got a bunch of socks I can't find mates for," Phoebe volunteered.

Phoebe handed three socks to Dalton, while Amy talked gently to Rowena.

"She's been through a lot," he worried.

"We have all been through a lot," Flo said.

"Now, very carefully, put the rats in the cage. *And don't let any get away!*"

Dalton hesitated. "You're never supposed to handle baby animals this soon."

"I know," Amy said reasonably, "but this is an emergency. We can't leave them where they are. Phoebe's parents aren't going to let any rat family live in her bed indefinitely. And what if one of them fell out of bed? The thing to do is for you to get them in the cage with as little handling as possible, and then not touch them again until they're older."

Dalton looked up at her. "You know rats better than anybody I ever met."

"Shut your door while you're transferring them." Flo stood in the hall, looking very, very weary. "Once they're all in the cage, count them, carefully, each of you. Then tie the cage door shut . . ."

"Oh, it locks," Dalton assured her.

"Tie it, too," she said.

Phoebe shut the door of her room.

"Rowena will just chew through anything that's not steel," Dalton told Amy.

"Ms. Norberg seems to be getting kind of tense," Tiffany observed. "I guess maybe being locked out took a troll on her."

"Took a troll?" Amy asked.

"She means toll," Phoebe said.

Once Rowena and her babies were settled in

the cage, Dalton let out a long breath. "They seem pretty calm." He looked at Amy. "Would you consider going steady with me?"

While Amy explained that she wasn't going to go steady for years yet, Phoebe called through the door. "It's okay. All the rats are in the cage."

Flo did sound tense. "Now you come get the sleeping bags and take them in there."

Phoebe opened the door. "But Wolf is going to sleep in here."

"Wolf?" Flo was sitting on a chair with the pieces of telephone in her lap. *"What wolf?"*

"You know. Mr. Cubby, the sculptor. He calls himself Wolf Chandon. So if he sleeps in my room . . ."

"He won't." Flo rolled her head around, the way Iris did to relieve tension in her neck. "He left."

Phoebe was astounded. "But it's four o'clock in the morning! It's cold and foggy! And he didn't even take his stuff that the dog didn't eat!"

"He took his sculpture," Flo said.

Now Phoebe was truly worried. "You don't think it had anything to do with us, or the rats?"

"Take the sleeping bags," Flo told her.

"He'll have to come back for his stuff." But saying it didn't make Phoebe any more certain he would.

"He may, someday," Flo said. "I gave him my phone number."

Phoebe was astonished. "Do you think he likes

you?" Right away, she realized that was not the way to put it. "I mean — I didn't think he liked *anybody*." She thought for a minute. "You could just take his stuff upstairs tomorrow, so he could pick it up there if he comes around. That way . . ."

"That way, you're thinking, he may not tell your parents about all that happened here."

"If he doesn't see them for a long time, it might not even come up. Of course, they're going to ask what happened to the telephone. Letting him take the blame for wrecking it would be crummy." She looked at the phone pieces and clapped her hand over her mouth. "Oh, wow! The telephone! What if Heather's parents have been trying all night to call her here? If my folks called tonight, they'd just figure Wolf had left it off the hook."

"I'm sure if Heather's parents were deeply worried, they'd call the police. And if nobody was at their apartment, they'd have the police check out her other friends' houses."

It made sense to Phoebe. Also, it was a relief not to think they all had to rush back to Heather's in the cold, foggy dark. Besides, it was no kind of night to move rat babies. "Were you trying to fix the phone?"

"I was . . . hoping I could stick it together enough to use it."

"Did you need to call someone special?" Phoebe asked.

"Only a locksmith. Take the sleeping bags."

There was only one more crisis to be dealt with this night. Heather came into the study. "Ms. Norberg, what about the rug at my place?"

"Tell me again what you put on it," Flo said.

"Let's see." Heather looked at Amy. "Vinegar." She gazed at the rest of them. "Salt. Baking soda. Lemon juice. Detergent. And then it all started fizzing and hissing."

"I should think so."

"What's going to happen?"

"Oh, it fizzed and hissed itself out hours ago. In the morning, you can scrape off the mess with something like a piece of stiff cardboard. You can try plain water on the rest. Then blot it as dry as you can."

"Will it leave a spot?" Heather asked anxiously.

"Probably," Ms. Norberg said.

10

Phoebe woke feeling groggy and tired. She peered at her clock.

Nine! She sat up.

There were people talking in another room.

Barefoot, struggling into her robe, she padded into the living room. Had Heather's parents gotten so frantic they called the police? Had Ms. Norberg been wrong about the rug settling down, so wrong the fire department had to quell it? Had Wolf been found wandering with *The End of Being* down some dark, dangerous street?

Flo Norberg sat on an easy chair cradling a cup between her hands, her feet tucked under her. Iris and Brian sat on the sofa across from her, Iris trying to detach one key from a chain.

Too late, Phoebe thought. If they see me duck back into my room they'll figure I have something to hide. If I just had a few minutes to figure out what they were going to say, I'd have an idea what I should say.

"Here you go." Iris got up and handed the key to Flo. "I'm so sorry. I don't know what I was thinking . . . what I was *not* thinking . . . taking it with me. It's so fortunate the children were here to let you in."

"Actually, W — " Flo began.

"You just never know with Wolf," Iris said. "He might as easily have turned you away." She saw Phoebe. "There's my lamb."

Brian smiled. "And wasn't she the brave, smart girl to bring everybody over here when Heather's sitter canceled out? She knew she could count on you, sick or well," he told Flo.

Iris held out her arms to Phoebe. "This child has always had remarkably good judgment, and such presence of mind." As soon as Phoebe came within range, Iris drew her down on the sofa. "Anyone else would have been devastated to find a rat giving birth in her bed. Poor, dear Wolf. I'm afraid children and rodents are just too unsettling a combination for him to cope with."

She told! Phoebe thought. Flo Norberg told my parents everything! And they're not even upset! They're even pleased with me! What a slant Ms. Norberg must have put on it.

Iris patted Phoebe's shoulder. "Why don't you wake your friends, dear. I'll run out for a new telephone while your father makes his pancakes with lichee nuts, and then we'll go over and do what we can for the rug. I wonder if ginger root would settle poor Chihuahua's stomach. It's wonderful for humans."

"I called your apartment and left a message that you were here," Brian told Heather at breakfast. "They called back a little while ago. They just got in."

Heather stopped poking at her pancakes. "Are they mad?"

"Of course not." He passed the green tomato chutney to Flo. "They were very proud of you for having the initiative to bring everyone over here where Ms. Norberg could look after you. They just wanted me to ask you what happened to the rug."

The place seemed still and empty, especially with Amy gone. Phoebe felt almost lonely, with the rest of Sunday to fill, and nothing to fill it with. That's one of the problems with being an only child, she thought.

When the phone rang, she hurried to answer. To her surprise, it was Tiffany.

"Were Heather's folks very worried?" Phoebe was cautious. Tiffany had never telephoned her before just to be friendly.

"Her folks," Tiffany said, "didn't even try to call all night. Parents are basically *oblivious*, do you know that?"

"And what about the rug?"

"We scraped all the stuff off and blotted it."

"I mean, are they furious?"

"No. Mrs. Bowen said, 'Do you blame the kid for not watching the dog, or the dog for eating the casserole, or the klutz who left the casserole where the dog could get it?' "

"They must have had a great time at the festival, to take everything so well," Phoebe reflected.

"Yeah. So did you ask your folks about taking a rat?"

"I'm going to wait a little and see how upset they are when Wolf doesn't come back. I don't think Ms. Norberg told them all about Chihuahua and Rowena, and I don't see any point in bringing it up until somebody else does."

"Wolf hasn't even called?"

"Not since my mom brought home the phone."

"Heather's folks went out to rent a rug-cleaning machine. I figure I'll wait until we see how the rug turns out before I ask about getting a rat. So I'll see you, okay? It was a really interesting weekend. Oh, listen. Dalton wants Amy's phone number. He wants to know if she'll promise to get engaged when they're older."

"Tell him he should call her in maybe another eight or ten years. Don't hurt his feelings. Say that her parents are very strict and old-fashioned, which they might be, for all we know."

After she hung up, Phoebe sat thinking things over. There was only one enormous worry left.

Sooner or later, her parents would wonder why Wolf was still gone after all of the kids went home.

Brian looked in. "Scrabble?"

Iris was setting a tea tray on the coffee table in the study. Brian opened the trunk in the corner and got out the Scrabble set.

"See?" Sitting on the floor, Iris poured a cup of blackberry tea. "Now aren't you glad that Tiffany and Dalton and Rowena came?"

Phoebe stared at her. "Mother, *why*?"

Brian set out the Scrabble on the coffee table. "If they hadn't, Wolf would undoubtedly be with us yet."

"Wait a *minute*!" Phoebe was stunned, dumbfounded. "You invited him. You were after us all the time not to upset him. You sent us to the *fair* because of him!"

Iris handed her a cup of blackberry tea. "You see, dear, you never really know a person until you've had him around your house. Just sharing a warehouse, we only saw Wolf as difficult. Having him here even for a short time, we realized he is impossible."

Iris passed her a platter of fortune cookies. "If it hadn't been for you children and Rowena, I don't know what we would have done. We could hardly have asked him to leave without devastating him, after all he'd been through. Poor wretch. I just thank goodness he left of his own accord. Otherwise it would have been so awkward sharing the warehouse with him again."

"But, Mama," Phoebe cried, "aren't you worried that you might never see him again?"

"Oh, he'll drop by," Brian said with serene confidence. "He'll need to borrow money."

Phoebe broke open her cookie. She didn't bother reading the fortune. Her parents had bought the cookies at The Far East Trading Company distress sale, and so far every one had had the same fortune in it.

"Sweetheart," Iris asked her, "how would you feel about having one of those little rats for your very own? That way we won't have to worry that Wolf might take a notion to come back for a stay. You could go pick one out after lunch. I'm just sorry Rowena had a litter. There are few good homes for rats, you know."

Sitting on the floor, her back against the sofa, waiting to finish the game and go get her rat, Phoebe took stock of her life. She had no brother, no sister, no aunts or uncles, not even a cousin. She had only two parents and a grandmother she seldom saw.

Iris laid her tiles, one by one, perpendicular to Brian's first word, *tea.* "X-A-N-T-H-I-C," she spelled out.

Brian smiled at her proudly.

Phoebe looked at her parents fondly. They are

odd. They even forget they're supposed to be playing Scrabble *against* each other. But they suit me. And sipping blackberry tea while playing Scrabble is about the coziest way I can think of to spend the time before I pick out my rat.

Kids in a three- or four-child family, she reflected, must have to live with a lot of stress. I guess I'm just lucky.